THE HORSE ON THE SIDEWALK

"*The Horse on the Sidewalk* is the best kind of coming-of-age tale, one full of peril and heroism and young love. Interconnected stories reveal Gil Wheeler, a boy becoming a man in postwar Albuquerque, boom years when the city sprawled and young men craved motorcycles. A flawless snapshot of a time and a place worth remembering."

—**Steve Brewer**, author of *Trouble Town*

"These short stories delight the reader with their minimalist precision, their eccentric humor, and the off-the-wall details of their no-bull realism. Baker Morrow has become one of my favorite storytellers."

— **V. B. Price**, author of *Albuquerque: A City at the End of the World*

"No accident that young Gil Wheeler is the scrappy 'wheel-man' of the far east mesa suburbs of the Duke City. Readers will brace for all the scooter lore under heaven with the Cushman Eagle flying over them all. These stories capture boom-town Albuquerque in its first explosion."

—**Enrique Lamadrid**, author of *Water for the People*

"These short stories, set in post-WWII Albuquerque, have a vein of innocence running through them, which Morrow brings to the surface with his pitch-perfect dialogue. Listen to these pages: the kids (as well as the alleged adults) are living each messy day as they find it. What a delight."

—**Carl Mayfield**, author of *Sandia Mountain Sequence*

THE HORSE ON THE SIDEWALK

stories

BAKER H. MORROW

Casa Urraca Press

ABIQUIÚ

Author photograph by Kristina Werenko.
Set in Baskerville URW with touches of Baskerville.

First edition

27 26 25 24   1 2 3 4 5 6 7

ISBN 978-1-956375-32-9
Ebook ISBN 978-1-956375-27-5

CASA URRACA PRESS

an imprint of Casa Urraca, Ltd.
PO Box 1119
Abiquiú, New Mexico 87510
casaurracapress.com

To Jim and Val Laffoon

Contents

A Note of Introduction

ALBUQUERQUE, NEW MEXICO, is an old commercial town that was founded as a Spanish colonial villa in 1706. It's only three years younger than St. Petersburg, Russia, founded by the flashy Czar Peter the Great in 1703.

Albuquerque turned into a boomtown after World War II, urged on by the less grandiose Mayor Clyde Tingley, and it tacked on forty or fifty square miles of new city in only fifteen or twenty years. The postwar developers couldn't build fast enough, especially in the Northeast Heights at the foot of the Sandia Mountains, and new families from all points of the compass set up their lives in neighborhoods whose history was often marked in months, not years.

I was just a kid in those days, but even the kids understood that we were all part of something fresh. Our parents talked endlessly about how they had lived their early lives during the Depression and the Second World War, but they lived now in this new place and I think they were glad to have it. The Northeast Heights had a shiny,

original feeling of just-built permanence, and we had a notion about those times that they just might last.

The physicist Carlo Rovelli, who thinks a lot about the idea of time, talks about this idea. "We inhabit time as fish live in water," he says.

I think, too, that we can't do without the rich sentiment of time. Maybe we want to believe that whatever there is has always been, and that it will never end.

But of course that's just wishful thinking. The kids in those once-new places grew up, the just-finished streets developed potholes and their streetlights burned out and were only sometimes replaced, and the suburbs and their houses and gardens weathered the relentless years and acquired a bit (quite a bit) of the patina of age.

What's left? Photographs in someone's shoeboxes and albums, in the back of a closet or in archives. And stories, of course.

THE HORSE
ON THE
SIDEWALK

I

On the Mesa

THIS GUY'S NAME was Ray, and he had a BSA.

I think it was a 250cc, but it could have been bigger. It made a great sound, and you never saw him going anywhere without his girlfriend Leah on the back.

The sound of the pipes, of course, came from the fact that the BSA was a four-stroke. That kind of engine didn't need the pint of oil that you had to pour into the gas tank every time you filled up, which was exactly what you had to do with a two-stroke like a Vespa or a Lambretta. Those motors were semi-cool—maybe not totally uncool. A bike was totally uncool.

But this guy Ray didn't have to worry about that. He wore La Parot Pomade on his hair. He drove around in his big Buddy Holly bat-wing glasses with his girlfriend on the pillion and her long blonde hair streaming out behind and her arms around his waist and he didn't have a care in the world.

He sat across from me in English.

"What are you reading?" he said.

"Now?" I said.

"No, man. Not now. For that report she wanted."

"*The Voyage of the Beagle*," I said.

"I haven't looked yet. In the library. I don't want to read anything about dogs."

"It has to be something scientific. A book on the history of science."

I thought we were talking pretty quietly, but no.

"Stop, boys," said Mrs. Crook. "Come up here."

When we got to the desk, she said, "It's quiet time. As in 'quiet.'"

"Yes, ma'am. We were talking about our assignment."

"Less talking and more reading are what is called for, Gil," she said.

"Yes, ma'am."

"What is your book?"

I showed her the Darwin.

"The lead-up to the theory," she said.

"Yes."

"Mr. Dailey?" she said.

"Nothing yet," said Ray. "Maybe something about mechanics, or engines."

"I've seen you on that motorcycle, Ray," said Mrs. Crook, deadpan.

You never could read her. She was pretty stern, and she always kept you at arm's length. We were ants, and she was a tarantula.

"... with that Leah Barnes." She looked at Ray with her icy gray eyes. Then she looked at me.

"One more time," she said, "and you fellows are off to see Mr. Greene."

That, of course, was the principal.

"Why don't you go to the library?" she said. "Gil, you might help Ray pick something. You have fifteen minutes."

"Yes, ma'am."

As we went down the hall, Ray said, "Jesus Christ. How are we supposed to figure this stuff out if we don't talk? Jesus Christ."

I didn't want to go back to the principal's office. In general, he wasn't a bad guy. You could talk to him a little. But he had a big paddle and he would absolutely use it if he didn't sense some kind of promise in you. A direction. Or contrition. It was always a good idea to show both.

I am contrite, I practiced in my head, *and I'm going somewhere.*

The Early Reciprocating Engine: Its Origins and Development in Automobiles and Two-wheeled Vehicles saved Ray. It was by Harlan C. Outs. Ray found it almost right away, after I pointed out the section to him. "This is good, man," he said. "Thanks."

Mrs. Crook looked up from her papers and frowned as we came back into class. Then she looked at her watch. "Ready by Monday, then?" she said. It was five days away.

"Ready," said Ray.

Part of the problem was that I had been in a little trouble only a month or so earlier—a slight scrap after class with this kid who knocked a bunch of books out of my hand in front of some girls and then threw my class notebooks skidding down the hall near the lockers. I took a swing at his face but he pulled back and I missed. I only hit him on the shoulder. He punched me in the jaw and it was a pretty good one and my right foot slipped and I went down. My head hit the locker as I fell—the door catch, actually—and I had a gash just behind my ear.

"What the hell are you little bastards doing?" said Mr. Postlethwaite, the science teacher. He grabbed this kid, who was a little squirt named Bobby Hiller, and shoved him up against the lockers. The girls ran. "Get his books," he said to Hiller. I got up and pressed a handkerchief against my ear.

Mr. Postlethwaite had a tight crewcut and a bow tie and he smelled like Aqua Velva. He had been in the Marines and you knew it was all he could do to keep from knocking our lights out.

"I just slipped," I said. My voice was level.

"He slipped," said that little crud Hiller. He was a little scared. It made me mad that this kid was so fast with his fists and he only came up to my shoulder.

"You should be an example," said Mr. Greene in his office. "Both of you. Especially you, Wheeler." He let us off with a warning. "One more time," he said, shaking his head, and we slipped out the door. Hiller and I walked back toward the big open locker room, and he pulled a mashed pack of Luckies out of his hip pocket, palming them till he got outside.

"I'll get you," he said, and he walked off. The inside of my cheek was sore where I had bitten it when he punched me.

I was walking down a dirt road at the edge of the mesa when I heard a motorcycle coming up fast behind me. It was a nice, cool afternoon with cotton-ball clouds over the mountains just to the east and a couple of dogs running through the grass on the plain a quarter-mile away. They looked like coyotes.

"Hey, Wheeler," said Ray, slowing down. He had Leah hanging on behind him. She spread her fingers out across his chest as he talked and she smiled at me. She had hazel eyes. She was trying pretty hard to look like she meant business.

"You want a ride on this thing?" he said. "Maybe drive it?"

"Sure," I said.

"IGA at ten o'clock on Saturday. Don't be late," he said.

Two days later I walked up to the IGA grocery at about 9:45. It wasn't very far—just up the block, really—and I liked the people who ran the place. The Griffins. They were polite to kids and sometimes friendly. The place was well stocked and they kept it clean. They acted like they knew what they were doing.

I liked the grocery business anyway, and the produce counters in particular. The Griffins kept their displays spotless, cold, and lit up, and the vegetables and fruits smelled good and were always crisp. Nothing soggy. There were drops of water on the heads of lettuce and the apples were shiny and cool when you touched them.

I thought with a lot of luck I could get on as a sacker sometime. Or maybe a stocker. I knew how to sweep floors and did it well from a lot of practice and maybe I could do that, too.

I bought a Coke from Mrs. Griffin, gave her a nickel deposit for the bottle, and sat down on the curb out front to drink it.

Dailey came up about ten minutes late. You could hear that beautiful BSA from two or three blocks away. The pipes were deep and rumbly.

"Gil," he said.

"Where's Leah?"

"Giving her mother a permanent in the sink," he said. "Takes all morning." He had chewed a toothpick down to a stub and he pitched it into the gutter. "Stinks like hell in that kitchen."

"My grandmother does that sometimes," I said.

"Hop on."

We shot up wide dusty Candelaria Road and Ray got the motorcycle into fourth gear just as we came to the intersection at Eubank Boulevard. That was a quick two-lane route, mostly asphalt, that ran south four or five miles to U.S. 66. Ray clipped down Eubank and hit sixty with no trouble. He paused only for the stop sign at Lomas.

"Watch for cops, kid," he said. "They know me here."

Sure, Ray.

There wasn't much traffic on Route 66, which was Central Avenue, unless you looked a few miles to the west, down toward Wyoming Boulevard. Just two or three curio shops scattered along the road, a bar, and, of course, the Terrace Drive-In. You could see it down there on the south side with the Lombardy poplars out front and lining the drives and the pretty Spanish dancer on the Central side of the screen. At night she kicked up her neon heels and lifted her elbow and a corner of her skirt.

Ray lit up a cigarette as we turned east toward Tijeras Canyon. There was just nothing out there. The city fell away behind us, and to the north the sand dropseed and sideoats grama ran across the mesa in waves stirred up by the wind as far as you could see. There were stands of cholla and snakeweed where the sheep had grazed too closely, and pink and white Apache plumes in the dry channels leading up to the base of the mountains. The foothills were a light brown and yellow, with little bits of green from the oaks and junipers, and you could see outcrops of granite everywhere. Above them the high Sandia Mountains were blue and, in the far distance, purple.

I didn't want to hang on to Ray like Leah did, so I gripped the underside of the seat with my fingertips. He wasn't particularly good with corners, taking them too fast and sometimes hitting patches of gravel, and he wouldn't put out his boot on the inside of a curve as he turned. I did. I was ready to kick the ground to steady us if we started skidding, but he didn't like that and he told me to knock it off.

Juan Tabo was a famous roller coaster road, up and down in continuous rolls, all dirt, and indifferently graded in all seasons. Ray turned onto it from Route 66 and shot north with his head cocked back at an angle. He was trying to look like James Dean or Marlon Brando, down to his white tee shirt and black jacket with a bunch of zippers and his black engineer's boots.

That English engine hummed and we just flew along, airborne as we came up over the ridges between the dry washes. Ray had his cigarette stuck in the corner of his mouth, being cool. The road was pretty straight and we did all right with the flying until a guy in a blue Ford pickup went by us going south at some speed and kicked up a lot of dust. The air got all thick with it and Ray couldn't see a groove worn out by water flowing crosswise right in front of him. He hit it hard, and the wheels slid out from under the BSA and it bounced and laid over on its side.

I sailed off the back and landed in the sand in the bottom of the arroyo. Ray burned his leg on one of the hot exhaust pipes and scraped up one arm of his leather jacket. He had grit in his messed-up hair and the left lens of his glasses was cracked. A big star crack.

The motorcycle only had a bent rearview mirror. He jerked it upright and wiped it off with a rag he had in his jacket pocket.

"Goddammit," he said.

I thought he looked a little shocked, but I had the wind knocked out of me, too, and I stood up and dusted off my pants. Then I sat down right away on a chunk of granite to get my breath.

Ray jiggled the carburetor buttons and fiddled with the screws and jumped on the starter. The motor caught after two or three kicks. He revved it.

"You walk, Wheeler," he said. "You did this."

"What the hell, Ray?"

"You walk. I'm a friend of Hiller's, anyway, and I don't like what you did to him."

"He started it, Ray," I said, but the guy was already over the hill and on to the next arroyo.

It took me two and a half hours to hike home across the mesa to the northwest. It was all downhill. Not too hard. I went cross-country, not following the roads, which were dusty and indirect, and as it was late October it wasn't too hot. I came out of it with just a split lower lip.

"Aren't you working today, Jim?" said my mother when I came in.

"Yeah," I said. My first name is James, which I like well enough, so naturally she sometimes called me Jim. Everybody else called me Gil from my middle name, and she was starting to do that, too.

"Get off early, Mom?" I said. She worked in a little clothes shop, although she was really a music teacher. Women's clothes.

"I'm going back," she said.

I could hear her rustling around in the kitchen while I was cleaning up in the bathroom, and when I came out she had a baloney sandwich with Miracle Whip and lettuce and a cup of tea for me.

My brother Lenny had already eaten half his sandwich. He was sitting at the kitchen table. "Nice lip," he said.

That English engine hummed and we just flew along

I was thinking about Dailey as I ate, and not very kindly, but mostly I didn't want to have to handle him at the same time as that pissant Hiller.

I had to go. "See you, Mom," I said. "Thanks." I was gulping the tea.

"Wait just a minute," she said. "I'll give you a ride down to the center. What's wrong with your mouth?"

Connie Francis had a new hit out that weekend. It was called "Fallin'." I heard it on Sunday afternoon on KQEO, 920 AM. She was falling into something with a boyfriend, and guess whose fault that was?

I loved it the first time I heard it. I was writing my paper on FitzRoy's ship, the *Beagle*, and its researches, which I finished even though I had to work that Sunday. I had the radio on the whole time, and Connie was a smash. They played that song again and again.

The corners of Mrs. Crook's mouth went up just slightly when I gave her the paper on Monday. She dipped her chin at me. It was eight pages, in my best handwriting, with only one or two small smudges and a single crossed-out word. I used an Esterbrook fountain pen that I had borrowed from my dad and I added references and footnotes.

There were a good thirty kids in that class, and it took her a while to rake in all the scholarly essays. Ray, of course, hadn't shown up that day.

"One salient fact," she said, once she had them. "You'll present them in one to two minutes each. I'll go alphabetically."

Salience.

By the time she got to me, the class period was almost gone.

"Mr. Wheeler," she said.

"Darwin rowed ashore from FitzRoy's ship all along the east coast of South America," I said. "Maybe hundreds of times. Probably dozens, though. He collected plant and animal specimens and fossils. Then he rowed back to the *Beagle* and catalogued everything."

Mrs. Crook looked closely at me. Then she glanced at the wall clock.

"He was always seasick," I said. "He never got over it."

The bell rang and I collected my stuff.

"It's hard to see how he did it," I said to her as everyone streamed out. "It was a wild place and he was massively uncomfortable."

In the hallway I ran into Leah with the very long hair.

"Ray's not here today," she said.

"I noticed."

"His brother's mad about the BSA."

"It was only the mirror."

"It was the tank, too," she said. "Scratches. And the frame is bent in the back."

That beautiful red motorcycle with the black frame and flaring chrome pipes. I hated to think of it.

"I have to get to class," I said.

"Me, too."

"Ray told me that was his motor," I said.

"Well, it's not. How would he pay for it? He doesn't have a job. His brother pounded the snot out of him."

"Bye, Leah."

"You have a job," she said. "That's what Jill told me."

She was talking about Jill Summers, my friend.

She stepped up and straightened my collar with two fingers. She smelled really good, kind of flowery. Then she pushed back the hair over my left ear. She touched my broken lip.

"He's not that cool," she said.

II

Wheels Make the Man

I HAD TO SOLVE a couple of problems, and due to my habits of mind I didn't like to think of them much until the afternoons. After school.

I got out of my last class, which was science, about 3:10 or 3:20, and I had to be at work by 4:30. The trouble was that I had to walk home first, and I tried to do that with nonchalance in the company of this pretty blonde who lived just down the street from me. Her name was Marian Calvert, and she was just gorgeous.

"Come over about seven-thirty," she said. "We'll do science."

We sat in her dining room with her dad scowling at me across a long brick planter full of airplane plants. It stood between us and where he was sitting with his feet up on the coffee table in front of the TV in the living room.

"Keep it down in there," he said, looking daggers at me. He liked to watch *The Untouchables*. Chicago gangsters from the twenties. Robert Stack, Bruce Gordon, and Nehemiah Persoff.

So did I, but Marian was more fun than Eliot Ness.

We went over chemical formulae and book chapters on geology and atomic weights, and her mom brought us glasses of lemonade and Pecan Sandies.

Marian winked at me during these sessions, and that evening she put her hand on my knee after her mom had gone back into the kitchen.

A stranger sensation I have never had. Nor a stronger.

My voice was just starting to crack that semester and it sometimes went down in register for a few minutes at a time, and I kept looking in the mirror for something besides fuzz on my upper lip. I had a distinct new hair or two on my chest, discovered after a spell of hard searching, and I had grown maybe an inch. But her hand on my kneecap got a fast stir out of me and I had to catch my breath. She kept it there for maybe half a minute and her eyes danced.

So much for Marian and evening study hall.

If I was lucky enough to catch her at her locker after school there were these other guys after her too, milling around, never knowing how to talk to her, and she and her friends liked all that attention. So you had to wade through them and not look too eager or too stupid, both of which took effort and skill, and then you always had to wait for one of Marian's girlfriends to come back from her homeroom or the can before you could leave with her. With *them*, actually.

For that matter, I didn't know how to talk to her, either. I just said simple things like, "Do you want a Coke?" and hoped for the best.

All of this took time, and I was nervous. If I didn't get home to drop off my books and class notes and then get to work at Huttontown Shopping Center by 4:30 or 4:45, I was in for a great deal of trouble.

But Marian, of course, was irresistible. She had blue eyes and long lashes and a swelling brand-new chest under those lacy white blouses. Thin ankles. And she had a sweet, if misleading, voice.

My friend Harold Claus had a fast yellow Cushman Eagle, and he would often give me a ride if I wasn't walking with Marian. First home, where I would leave a note for my brother, and then on to work. Harold had his own afternoon paper route in Bel Air, a few miles west of our junior high, and he would drop me off on his way.

I sold the same afternoon paper, but on the streets. I was the street paper guy.

It came about like this:

The summer before, I had no problems getting around. I was fresh out of seventh grade at another junior high and I was riding a three-speed English racer that had been perfectly okay in grade school. But it had no cachet whatsoever beyond that. You couldn't ride a bike to junior high.

Never mind that it was tough and fast and I liked it. How would you ever impress a girl like Marian Calvert with a green, thin-tired Schwinn when guys like Harold had Cushman Eagles?

Eagles not only looked good, they sounded great. They had solid four-stroke engines, very throaty, and a two-speed shift on the left side of the tank just like what you would find on a Harley 74—one of those big hogs you saw going around.

But kids could drive Eagles because they were under five horsepower, and the license you could get when you were thirteen worked for them. You could crank them up to sixty or sixty-five even with the little wheels. Another guy who owned one said his did seventy-five or eighty, but

Harold and I doubted it. His name was Bill Pike, he was a ninth-grader, and he was prone to exaggeration.

At any rate, you might say that an Eagle was my goal.

I pedaled the green racer to the swimming pool a lot of times that summer, leaving it in the rack just outside the gate with all the other bikes. The pool was right off Menaul Boulevard near the shopping center, which was the biggest in the far Northeast Heights, and it was built in the shape of a giant capital A. In fact, it was called the "A" Pool. Everyone went there. The water was bluer than the sky from the tiles, and cold.

My friends and I finished swimming one day and took showers and went out through the gates and the green bike was gone. Just like that. All the other bikes were there.

Don, the guy who owned the place and always saw everything, was at the front window cage.

"Did you see anyone on a green bike, sir?" I asked. "An English racer?"

"Hang on a second," he said. He sold a couple of tickets to a man and his wife who had just walked up.

"A green bike," I said. "I was here for about an hour and now it's gone."

He thought for a few seconds.

"You always seem to see everything," I said.

"I didn't see that. I didn't see anybody take your bike." He shook his head sideways.

"Nobody hanging around?" I said.

"No one."

This pool owner looked a lot like Rod Serling, the *Twilight Zone* guy. He even gritted his teeth like Serling when he talked.

"Can I leave my name in case it turns up? It's Gil Wheeler."

*How would you ever impress a girl when guys like Harold
had Cushman Eagles?*

His brows knitted, and he laid his cigarette on an ashtray that sat on the sill. "Just check back later," he said.

It wasn't the first time this had happened to me. A kid swiped my earlier bike off the school grounds when I was about ten and I saw him going up an alley half a block away and chased him down and got it back. I was just firm with him and there was no punching necessary.

But this was different. There was no one to chase. My friends went off on their own bikes and I walked home.

"Well, that's a shame," said my dad when I told him. "That's too bad." He was watching a golf match on the tube with a second or third whiskey in his right hand. He drank it neat. There were five stubs in the ashtray and he had another one going. Old Golds. His words came out a little thick.

"Where's Mom?" I said.

He stared at the screen.

I was thirsty and drank some lemonade out of the pitcher in the refrigerator.

"Mom?" I said, when I came back.

"At work," he said. His eyelids were heavy and his mouth was open a little.

I walked the mile and a half back to the pool and got there about 5:30. The place was quiet. And empty. The doors were open in front, there was no one in the ticket window, and the service gate, just off to one side of the bike rack, had swung back. I walked past it.

Nobody in the pool. Around the edges you could hear the return jets spurting softly into the still water. Don, the pool owner, sat sideways on the deck end of the low board, smoking. His neck looked very red from the sun. The phone rang and rang in the office and he didn't answer it. He looked up.

"Excuse me," I said. "I just came to check on the bike."

"The green one," he said. "Sorry. No sign of it." He took a big drag off his cigarette. "We're closed."

"It's early, isn't it?"

"Look," he said, "somebody drowned. She drowned."

"Oh, man. Who?"

"She did. Sarah Johnson. They called her Sally."

I knew her. She was a friend of some cousins of mine. Sally Johnson. She went to Ridgeline, my new junior high.

I stood there and looked out at the pool. One of the lifeguards' umbrellas tilted crookedly from its high perch.

"He left for a couple of minutes to go to the bathroom, and when he came back she was in the bottom at the deep end." Don the owner lifted his fingers toward the lifeguard's chair. Then he put his cigarette down and wiped his right cheek. "I called his brother to come and get him after the firemen and the ambulance left. It wasn't his fault, you know," he said.

"No," I said.

Sally Johnson. Brunette and tiny. With a pug nose.

"It was mine," he said.

Well, measured against the drowning of that poor Sally, the loss of the green bike was nothing.

Still, it was hard to get around. That was my second great problem.

I had bought the bike myself in the fifth grade out of money I had made selling greeting cards and seeds. I read an ad in the back of a comic book for the American Seed Company. Some guy named Uncle Harry was offering prizes or cash to kids who would go door-to-door hawking his products. I sent the ad in and everything turned out just as promised.

"Good afternoon, sir," I would say as the man of the house came to the door in his undershirt. "I'm selling seeds for the American Company."

People were mostly amused. Most of them were friendly, too. "What are they?"

"Carrots, lettuce, spinach, and onions," I said. This was in the spring, of course. "Or flowers. I have snapdragons, marigolds, and coleus. It has nice leaves."

"What does?"

"The coleus."

"Oh."

"A dime a pack. Six for fifty cents. And I have cards, too."

I often sold six packets of seeds at a time, and Uncle Harry let you keep half the money. You just sent the rest in. Not a bad deal. If you didn't want to keep the money he would send you prizes.

At first my mother, Kay, walked along to keep an eye on me. But after a while, she just let me go. I went block-to-block. "Be back by five," she said. "No later. Dinner's at six. And don't go too far."

I sold enough seeds to get one of Uncle Harry's pup tents, which I put to good use in the backyard and, a couple of times, in the mountains. But then I just started to hang on to the money. I opened up a little savings account at the bank with my mom's help and after a while I had a hundred dollars in it.

The bike was thirty, and though my dad was going to get it for me he was short when the day of the purchase came around.

"I'll pay you back," he said, but it was the last time I ever saw that thirty bucks.

So, a few months after the bike was swiped and poor Sally drowned, I was walking fast after school to get down to my job.

I was glad to find it because I didn't like depending on people for any length of time. Some people, anyway. It wasn't particularly wise.

"Look, Gil, just buy me some gas once in a while," said Harold. "It's not a problem. Hop on."

But I knew Harold had to throw his papers and then go out and collect. He didn't have a lot of time and he had to fit it in before dark. You had to go door-to-door in those days and squeeze the money out of your customers. "It's best if you can get a month or two out of 'em at a time," said Harold. He would collect the dollars and tear a few weekly coupons out of his book, which he gave to the homeowners as receipts. But it came to a little under two bucks a month, and people often had only a buck and a half or seventy-five cents. Sometimes Harold could hear the TV going and they wouldn't answer their doorbells. Then he just had to turn around and come back a week later.

This sort of thing was tedious. But how else could Harold pay his paper bill when the route manager showed up? You had to do that twice a month.

My own bills for selling that same afternoon paper on the street were due once a week. My route manager was a worried-looking but nice woman named Mrs. King, and she had hired me over the phone.

I had read a notice in the want-ads for somebody to sell papers at the shopping center and at intersections for two or three hours, six days a week, in the afternoon. The job appealed to me because it was early September and classes were just starting. The money would come in handy.

"Do you have any experience?" she said, when we met for the first time. She was dressed in jeans and a plaid shirt and she had her hair gathered up in a bandanna like a lot of women her age. It looked like a turban. She wore brown penny loafers, and she drove a half-ton Ford pickup. Light blue.

"Yes, ma'am," I said. "I've sold seeds and cards."

She smiled a little. "Good," she said. "Do you have good grades?"

"Yes, ma'am. For the most part. At least I did at my old school. I'm starting eighth grade at Ridgeline Junior High."

"Oh. That new one down Half Moon Street. Right at the edge of the mesa."

"Yes, ma'am."

"Do you have a watch?"

"No, I don't."

"Your name is Gil?"

"Gil Wheeler. James Gilbert Wheeler, actually."

"Well, Gil Wheeler, the papers sell for seven cents apiece and you get a half-cent. How many can you sell in an afternoon?"

"I can sell a hundred," I said, thinking three bucks a week sounded good. I had school expenses coming up.

"I'll give you fifty," she said. "My best boys sell maybe seventy-five downtown or over by the university. Buy a watch with what you make soon. I need you here at four-thirty every day. On the dot."

"Yes, ma'am."

"Three-thirty on Saturday."

I lifted up the stack of papers and looked at the headlines. The governor was visiting Quebec, and some Swiss Boy Scouts were paddling down the whole length of the Rio Grande.

"You'll make your money off tips. You can keep all of those. See all these stores?"

We were in the front parking lot of the center, under the big arching erector-set sign. She waved a rolled-up newspaper at the shops.

"Ask the store owners if you can leave a stack of papers next to their front doors. People will pay and leave the money on top of the pile."

"Okay."

"Then you go out to those islands"—she pointed at the medians on Menaul and on Wyoming—"and you sell the rest to people waiting for the light to change as they drive home."

"Got it."

"That's fifty." She looked at me for a moment. Then she peeled off five more and made a note in her canvas-backed book. I tucked in my shirt tail.

"Fifty-five," she said. "See you tomorrow at four-thirty."

I sold fifty-three papers, which made Mrs. King happy. The other two were from inside the stack, crumpled and torn, and I gave them back to her for credit. I also made $3.50 in tips. She gave me sixty-five papers and I got out on the medians, held them up so the drivers could read the headlines, and sold those, too.

Now I could think about getting a Cushman Eagle or some other real wheels. Maybe a Ducati Bronco.

Marian and I also did well, for a while.

One Saturday morning I went down the block to see her. Her mom was out. So was her dad, and her little brother was playing in the front yard. She was babysitting.

"Come in, Gil," she said. She smiled while she was chewing her lower lip. "Want a Coke?"

"Sure," I said. It was about eleven o'clock.

As I was drinking it, she said, "You're not supposed to be here. My folks are gone."

"I'll go," I said.

"Not quite yet," she said. We were sitting on the front room couch and she put her hand on my knee again.

We started to make out a little. Then a lot.

Neither one of us had much experience and we had to lean back a few times to figure out where our noses were supposed to go. If you leaned straight in, your nose got squashed. And eyes: were you supposed to close them right away? I thought so, but I caught her peeking at me in the middle of a big smacker.

Still, it was terrific. It made you gasp.

So we went on with our kissing practice—you could sure get lost in it—and after a while this little voice outside the window said, "Hi, Mom." We hadn't heard the motor.

"Oh, Jesus," said Marian. "Quick, out the back."

She really didn't have to tell me. I was through the kitchen, across the yard, over the wall, and into the neighbor's tomatoes in a few seconds. It was actually a tidy little peach orchard with tomato plants in lines between the trees, all going yellow in the early fall. I looked around: no neighbor. I shot down the fence line and went over the sidewall and was out into the next street in another ten seconds. I looked over my shoulder and went off down the sidewalk. It was another block and a half before I caught my breath.

Huttontown in those days was brand-new. In the east end, where the lustrous Marian and I lived, the houses were mostly concrete block with pitched roofs. One-car garages or carports. "Sort of ranch-style," my dad said. Maybe Modified Block-Ranch. They had two or three bedrooms but they weren't particularly big. They sat back from their new streets on large lots, though. People planted new trees—mostly elms, but some honey locusts and maples, too. A sycamore here and there. And they put in pines and spruces and grass and fruit trees and a lot of clunky arborvitae.

The houses on the west end were brick and bigger. Single-story. They were fresh and neat and dapper-looking.

Well, not a few of the new homeowners were out tending their baby trees and lawns as I walked by. They had little garden plots, with vegetables and rows of flowers. Since it was Saturday, two or three guys were washing their cars, with their kids helping them.

Boy, she's really something, I thought. My head was still racing. She did a trick with her tongue that made your brain light up. It was like a little minnow swimming around your mouth. I wondered when we might try all that again.

Not soon.

I went to a party a week or so later and there was Marian, dancing, pretty close, with Bill Pike, that ninth-grader with the allegedly fast Eagle. I just stood there for a couple of minutes and didn't move. I suppose I was staring at them.

"What are you looking at, kid?" said Pike. They were dancing to this Jørgen Ingmann song, "Apache." And Marian's friends were like twittering birds. They sat in the corner and looked at me and giggled.

"I just got here," I said to Pike.

Marian peered across Pike's shoulder at me, which wasn't hard to do since she was two or three inches taller than he was, and she cut me dead.

Their cheeks were touching, but she had to bend over quite a bit to make it work.

Marian's friend Darlene, who was one of the birds, slipped in beside me at the punch bowl. "She wants to ride, Gil," she said. "She doesn't want to walk."

True enough, I guess. But I had been putting some of that newspaper money in the bank, and as I walked back out into the night I knew it would add up to some kind of wheels in a few months. Maybe by spring.

III

Lost Among the Philistines

"WE LIVE in a suburb," said Salisbury.

He always sounded like he was twenty-five or thirty, twice as old as all of us actually were, and his voice had already changed to a smooth baritone. You wanted to pay attention to him.

"You think so?" said Jimmy Fitch.

"Sure," said Salisbury. He was purring. "Snow Heights is another one. So is Princess Jeanne Park."

"How do you know, Leo?" said Jimmy.

"What do you think a new subdivision is at the edge of a city?" said Leo. "It might as well be a new town. We're way the hell out here. I read about it in a book by a guy named Clarence Stein. My old man has it."

There was a drive-up hamburger stand called the Circle on Menaul down the way from Huttontown Shopping Center, and we were sitting at a wooden picnic table under some of its sheet-metal awnings eating cheeseburgers. It was raining, and pretty chilly. Menaul was a boulevard, but it had no trees in the medians, no parkways, and no sidewalks. Very raw. The Circle

29

was a godsend—you had to go a couple of miles west, down Menaul, to find another café of any kind. The cheeseburgers were thirty-five cents apiece and the Cokes and fries were a dime, so you couldn't do this sort of thing everyday.

"A suburb," said Jimmy. "No kidding."

We were all impressed—even Leo. We had heard of suburbs before, of course, but you found them in places like Long Island or New Jersey or Southern California. They showed up on TV—new houses in long rows. Nothing else in sight. In Los Angeles or Chicago, sure. Not New Mexico.

"Yup," said Leo. "New Mexico." He stuffed in a handful of hot greasy French fries. "We're a post-war suburb."

It was a new thought. We sat there munching, taking it in.

"Maybe you're right," said Jimmy. He was a tiny, sandy-haired kid—my age, but twenty pounds lighter. He hadn't grown yet. At all. "My dad opened up his body shop because he said people were running into each other out here and nobody in the Heights was doing that kind of work."

"Well, he's in for a surprise," said Salisbury. "Newton's uncle's gonna do the same thing." Leo was talking about this kid named Tommy Newton who was sixteen and pretty tall and had already flunked a grade or two. One of his pals from Jackson Junior High. He crammed in more of the French fries and threw a few onto the ground at the end of the table. Some little soggy sparrows flew down from their perches under the canopy and gobbled them up.

"I thought he was a mechanic at Jones Motors," I said. That was an old Ford dealership ten miles away on Central Avenue.

"He's been saving up," said Salisbury. "He's gonna make his move soon."

"What does he know about collision and body work?" said Jimmy. "My old man's as good as they come."

"Till now," said Leo.

"Oh, horseshit, Leo," I said. "How do you know all this?"

"I work with Newton, you know," he said, "on the rejects. Stuff they won't take down at the Ford place. At Newton's uncle's house."

Jimmy and I were both amazed that Leo could talk with so many fries crammed into his cheeks.

"I'm doing pretty well," said Salisbury. "Probably up to fifteen hours a week over at that place. It adds up, you know."

Well, maybe not too fast. Leo had a '55 or '56 Harley Hummer in his garage—mostly spread out across his dad's work table—and every time I went over to see him it was in the same condition. That is to say, no condition at all. Just pieces. He was rebuilding it.

"I'm getting new rings next week," he said. But no piston rings, or any other new parts, ever appeared. "It won't be long now." He had a factory poster of this cute official Harley-Davidson model up on the wall. She was a redhead in a bikini sitting on the driver's seat of a Harley 74 and pretending to rev it. "They'll do sixty," said Leo. He meant the Hummer, of course, not the 74, which would do twice that speed.

Unlike Leo, Jimmy had a real job. He swept the body shop out on Friday and Saturday nights, cleaned the cans, stocked parts, and helped out at the front desk. Sometimes he sanded down dents that had been filled in with Bondo. His sister Brenda worked there, too, at just about the same times as Jimmy. She was a junior at

Sandia High, a brand-new place a little west and north of Huttontown, and she was impossibly older and grown up and generally quiet. Sort of dignified and aloof. But Brenda would actually talk to us sometimes.

"Hello, Gil," she would say. "How's the paper business?"

"Just fine, Brenda," I said.

"Gary and I saw you on the island a couple of days ago," she said. "You had on your paper vest." She meant this canvas saddlebag that held lots of papers. It was like a poncho. You could put your head through it or drape it over the frame or the seat of a motorcycle. Gary was her boyfriend, a guy with a modified '32 Ford. She sat right next to him on the bench seat. Sometimes when they went by, Brenda had her arm across his shoulder. "He wants to know how you got that job."

"I applied for it."

"So did he. Two years ago. He didn't think it paid enough," she said.

Uh huh. As if sixteen-year-old punks could be choosy.

"Well, it does now," I said.

"He got on at K-W Auto Supply," she said. "He's the afternoon parts courier."

I didn't particularly like this guy Gary. He drove around in that flathead Ford trying to look like Robert Mitchum, knocking himself out to be cool.

Fitch's dad paid Jimmy something like seventy-five cents an hour. He was a regular employee. He paid Brenda, too, and he was a stickler about both of them working regular hours and being on time. He wasn't a bad fellow at all, but he was a little gruff. He was stiff in one leg—Jimmy said it was shrapnel or something from the war—and he liked to stand out on this concrete slab east of his shop and look at the Sandia Mountains and smoke. There was an elm tree that shaded it and he leaned against the trunk. I walked over to the place to see Jimmy after I finished with the papers one afternoon and Mr. Fitch nodded at me and kept on smoking.

"Hi, Gil," he said. He shook my hand and then looked at his palm. My hands were always dark with newsprint.

"Sorry, Mr. Fitch," I said.

"Don't be." He showed me his left palm, which was grimy from working on cars, and grinned.

He and Jimmy had been working for weeks on a go-kart in the back of the shop, and Jimmy chugged around the front of the place in it and stopped under the elm tree. It was quite an affair: gloss-black frame and body, low-slung, with a Briggs and Stratton four-stroke lawn mower engine and a red seat. "Stand on the frame behind me and hold on," said Jimmy. "Give me your bag." I gave him the canvas saddlebag with a few papers still in it. I had to crouch and lean forward to grab the steel tube roll-bar behind his seat. Jimmy put the saddlebag on the bed of the go-kart between his legs, revved the engine, and took off.

"Careful on Wyoming," said Mr. Fitch, but we barely paused at the edge of the road before we shot across. The power wheel was left-rear and it spat up gravel as Jimmy headed east up Claremont Avenue.

"How fast will it go?" I said.

"Maybe forty," he yelled, but we weren't doing that. Twenty seemed like sixty on that little go-kart. It was low—maybe an inch or two off the street, and it had no shocks. It jarred your teeth when you hit a bump. Jimmy lived just around the corner from me on McClellan Street, and we were there in five minutes. It was a *long* five minutes, really, because all I did was crane my neck looking for oncoming cars and cops.

"Thanks, Jimmy," I said, when he dropped me off. Jimmy's four wheels notwithstanding, I thought I would keep on saving my money for something with larger if fewer wheels, and shocks. Something higher off the road, too.

The newspaper business wasn't all just fun and games, plucking cherries off some tree with hanging branches and popping them into your mouth.

A friendly cobbler ran a shoe repair shop close to the middle of Huttontown Center, and when I asked him if I could leave some papers out front, he said, "Sure. Put 'em by the door there." I weighted them down with a large cobble and he let me keep it just inside the threshold at night. That was because I had lost a few papers to the wind only a day or two earlier.

There was a busy gift shop at the west end of the center and the owner of the place let me leave ten or so papers a day just outside his door. No problem at all.

After two weeks of this, I had collected some Vienna sausage cans and left them on top of the stacks of papers next to the cobbles for people to put their money in. It was better than having the coins scattered around.

I wanted to leave a pile of papers at the entrance to the drugstore, too, but the owner was never in when I tried to catch him to ask permission. I kept at it, though; I bought a little pocket watch there for two and a half bucks and the clerk at the cash register up front began to recognize me. "Hi, Gil," she said. "Mr. Cox went home early." She was a little nervous.

I worked my way up to eighty-five papers a day, selling most of them on the wide Menaul median at the Wyoming Boulevard intersection to people in their cars who were waiting for the light to turn green. They were eastbound—soon to be northbound—and headed toward their new brick houses with the stripling trees in Huttontown.

I watched the steady flow of cars and thought, *They're on their way to their new suburb.* They drove Fords and Chevies, mostly, with Plymouths mixed in. A few Mercs, too, and a Volkswagen now and then. Once in a while I saw some Dodge trucks and a Nash or a Packard. They headed north on Wyoming for two or three blocks and then peeled off to the east, running up the ascending streets as they made their way home. It was really just as Leo had said.

Sometimes I called out the headlines pretty loudly as I walked along those medians facing the cars. "Quemoy and Matsu shelled by the Chinese Communists," I yelled. Or, "Second anniversary of statehood celebrations in Alaska and Hawai'i." The paper was seven cents, but almost everyone gave me a quarter or fifty cents. Even at a dime I was making seven times the actual rate the publisher gave me.

But one Tuesday the papers were gone and the money was missing at the gift shop. Then it was the same thing on Wednesday at the shoe repair shop.

On Thursday a kid named Larry Pepper drove into the parking lot on his Cushman Two-Ten and parked about fifty yards away while I was picking up my papers from Mrs. King. He was a surly guy, always scowling. He was in my social studies class at Ridgeline Junior High. He had a flat face with puckered lips and he smoked like a chimney and indoors he smelled like old fumes. It was hard to be in the same room with him. Salisbury said his old man had bought him the Two-Ten, which was new and two-tone red- and cream-colored, with some "inherited money."

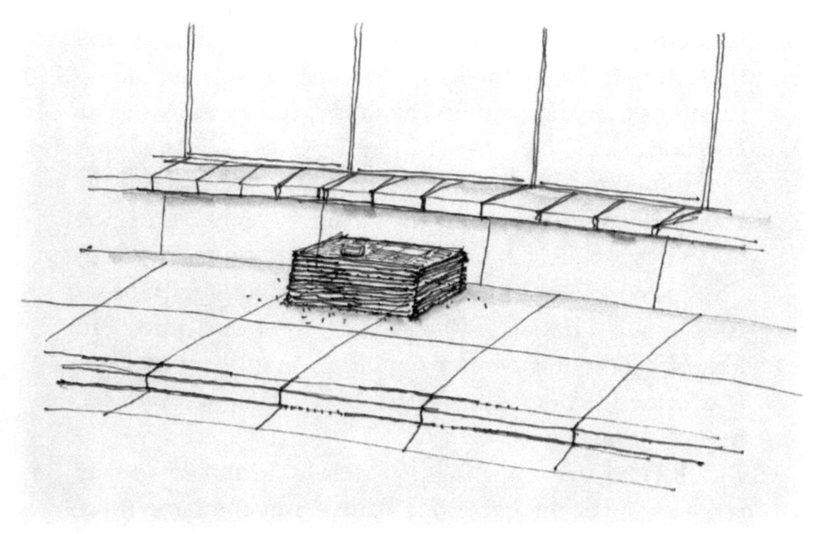

*I decided to take a chance and left a new pile of ten papers
on the sidewalk*

I tended to believe this, because there was no way that kid could get a job. He wouldn't try hard enough. He had flunked a grade in elementary school and been held back and he was not delighted about it.

Pepper was eyeing me and Mrs. King, and when I looked up from the papers and stared at him he kicked over his engine and drove off.

I left to set up my sales points. I had four of them—a pile each on the northbound and eastbound medians at the intersection, and a stack at each of the two friendly door entries in the shopping center. I decided to take a chance and left a new pile of ten papers on the sidewalk ten feet or so away from the front door of the Cox Apothecary.

Then I circulated: fifteen minutes on each of the medians, and afterward back to the stores. The shoe repair shop—it was called the Debonair—was my first stop. There were eight papers gone and all the money and my little can were missing. I went inside to see Mr. Simpson, the cobbler.

"Sorry to bother you," I said, "but did you see anyone hanging around?"

He put a boot down beside one of his lasts. "By your papers?"

"Yes, sir." He was a Black guy, one of the very few in New Mexico I had seen, and it was pretty exotic just to talk to him. He had a shine chair and cabinet and I had hit him up a few months earlier for a job polishing people's shoes.

"There was a kid who came up smoking maybe ten minutes ago," he said. "He bent over and I thought he was buying one of the papers. I didn't think anything of it. Somethin' happen?"

"Money's gone," I said.

He winced. "Saw him yesterday, too."

"I think I know that guy," I said. "Did he have black hair?"

"Yeah," he said. "Kind of scruffy."

"Thanks," I said. I turned to go.

"Cool off first," said Mr. Simpson. "Don't get too hot. He's a little bigger than you are." He flipped a shoe cloth over his shoulder. "Your name's Gil, right?"

"Yes, sir," I said.

"Well, remember, Gil," he said, "we are lost among the Philistines here. Watch yourself."

Outside, I straightened out the pile of papers, looked around, and left five more. I walked west toward the drugstore with my canvas paper bag hanging off one shoulder.

When I got there my pile of papers was thrown all over an empty parking bay and the change that had been on top of the stack was spread across the sidewalk. Mr. Cox stood beside his doorway and said, "Are you the little jerk who left those newspapers on the sidewalk?"

I thought he might take a swing at me so I watched him pretty closely. "Those are my papers, sir," I said. I tried to keep my voice level.

"Don't even think about picking up that change," he said. "I sell the newspaper inside, and I don't need the likes of you competing with me. That's my money. Or it should have been. You sold papers that I would have sold."

"No, sir," I said. I was picking up the papers and the change as fast as I could. "Those are my papers, and that's my money."

"And you didn't ask first."

I was about to tell him that I had tried, but he got very red in the face and said, "I oughta call the cops."

He was about to say more, but just then a man in a gray suit and his sleek wife got out of a big black Lincoln and walked toward the door of the drugstore. They heard Cox yelling and they stopped and stared at him. Then they looked at me.

Mr. Cox straightened up and pushed his hair back from his forehead.

I finished picking up my money and got the papers stuffed into the canvas bag. Mr. Cox looked at the man in the suit and then looked back at me. I was still pretty mad about Chapman and his little stunt.

"There's no call for you to use that kind of language with me, Mr. Cox," I said. "I can take a hint. You won't see me around here again."

"You can take a powder," said Mr. Cox. "That's what you can take."

I walked off toward the gift shop, and as I passed the guy in the gray suit he and his wife turned on their heels and went back to the Lincoln.

I didn't think my crime was big enough for Mr. Cox the pharmacist to be intolerably rude, if you want to know the truth of it. I won't change my mind about that.

It still wasn't that bad a day. I made a ton in tips out on the medians and sold all but three of my papers, although that meatball Gary, Brenda Fitch's boyfriend, drove by too fast in his '32 Ford and flipped a cigarette out the window in my direction. He was looking back at me to see the effect as he went around the corner and he hit the far curb with his right rear wheel. He overcorrected and the Ford jumped the street edge and went into the Wyoming frontage road. A guy heading south in a Studebaker swerved and honked at him, but Gary just kept on going.

I wrapped up for the afternoon and crossed the street to the Cosden Oil station to get a Coke before I walked home. The manager was a blond-headed guy named Del just back in the Heights after a couple of years in the Army. He didn't mind if I sat on a wire crate by one of the lube bays to drink the pop, so I put the canvas paper bag down and leaned back against the wall. I had to figure out what to do with that worthless Pepper.

I didn't have long to figure. Pepper drove up to one of the pumps on his Cushman. He killed the engine, took a drag off his cigarette, and lifted the nozzle off its hitch. He started to fill his tank. Then he took another drag and smirked as he looked in my direction.

"Know how I'm gonna pay for this, kid?" he said. He reached into the pocket of his jacket and pulled out my Vienna sausage can. He shook it over his head, jingling the coins. "Of course, a two-bit dumbass like you wouldn't know what to do about it."

My best chance with a guy like Pepper, who outweighed me by about fifteen or twenty pounds, was to punch him in the voicebox. That would make him choke, and then one or two more of the same would be the end of it.

But I'm nearsighted, so I took my glasses off and laid them carefully on the crate. I walked over to meet him and he came around the Cushman toward me. He was still smirking. I think.

I punched him as hard as I could but I was high. I missed his voicebox and caught him square in the nose and the upper lip. He looked surprised because I did it very fast, and he put his hand up to his nose. So I hit him once more for good measure. Side of the head. Real hard.

He took a step or two back.

"Give me my money," I said.

Now he was breathing hard.

"Give it to me."

He was backing up and his nose was bleeding onto his shirt.

"And the can, goddammit," I said.

"Holy cow, kid," he said.

"The name is Gil," I said. "Gimme the money, Larry."

He reached in his pants pocket and pulled out three or four ones and then a whole handful of change. He fished the sausage can out of his jacket and put all the money in it and handed it over.

Del the station manager had heard the commotion and he came up. He saw Larry's cigarette, still burning, on the ground by the pump.

"Who's smoking out here?" he said. He looked at Larry. "That yours?"

Larry wiped his nose with his sleeve and looked down.

"You owe me a buck-fifty," said Del. He rubbed out the butt with his heel.

Larry's fat lower lip was quivering. He stuck his hand in his pocket. "I'm out," he said. "He's got it."

"That true?" said Del. He looked at me.

"Nope," I said. I had the bills in my hand. "This is my money, Del."

"Look harder," said Del.

Larry reached into his left front pocket and dragged out two ones.

"Here's your change," said Del. He gave Larry a fifty cent piece. "Now get out of here."

I went back to the crate to retrieve my glasses and the saddlebags and Del followed me. "Don't fight around here, Gil," he said. "I'll lose business, and you won't be able to come back."

"I'm sorry," I said. "That guy lifted a bunch of my newspaper money over at the center. I apologize."

"No more," said Del.

"Sure, Del," I said. I put the Coke bottle back in the wire empties holder on the side of the machine.

It was getting dark, and as I walked home I shook my right hand a few times to see if I could get the numbness to go away. My second and third knuckles were notched neatly where Pepper's teeth had gone through the skin. I could not have hit the guy one more time with that hand.

It was just as well. I had been pretty lucky with Pepper—he hadn't brought along any of his friends. I was sure he had some, and I thought I would hear from them. But I did have my money back.

Jimmy and I had English with Mrs. Crook that fall, and we were reading parts of the *Iliad* the next morning in class. Hector Breaker of Horses was flinging his bronze spear at the Achaeans, splitting their foreheads open or smashing through their jaws and sending their teeth flying out of their mouths.

"At the dawn of Western Civilization," said Mrs. Crook. She was a gray-haired woman in her late forties, and she wore gray sweaters and gray flannel skirts. "These were Mycenaean people."

Achilles was sulking in his tent. Dead swordsmen and their yellow armor were strewn all across the Plain of Troy. Did these guys expect this sort of thing when they sailed east to the end of the wine-dark sea?

"And what about the gods, Jimmy?" said Mrs. Crook. "What do they have to do with this?"

"They're strange," said Jimmy. He had read a lot the night before. "They take sides, and they're mean."

To me he leaned over and said, "Pepper looks like he walked into a door."

Mrs. Crook said, "Nothing has changed much, has it? I mean, sixty or seventy million people died in that last war of ours. A horrible thing. World War Two."

We all knew about that. Our dads had come back from fighting it.

"And what was behind this Trojan War? Jeff?"

"A girl," said Jeff Stahl, another friend of mine. "The prettiest girl in the world. The Spartan queen. And money, I'll bet. Loot."

"Anything else?" said Mrs. Crook.

"And honor," said Jeff.

Salisbury caught up with me near the IGA store as I walked home. "They're talking about you," he said.

"Who is?"

"They are. Newton, for one. He's a good friend of Pepper's."

Newton was really a would-be hood, like Pepper. A punk. Salisbury said he was about to get his first car.

"So who's paying for it?" I said.

"I told you, man. He and I are both working for his uncle."

"How's the motorcycle, Leo?"

"Almost there. I'm gonna bore the cylinder next week."

"I've got to get to work," I said.

"Tell you what," said Salisbury. "I'll intervene on your behalf." He looked down at my right hand.

"I'll let you know, Leo," I said, and I waited for a break in the traffic to cross Candelaria Road.

IV

Stuck Up

I barely knew this kid—Richard Bontine—but he sent me a note in speech class just to get a rise out of me.

Dear Chicken Shit, it said. *If you got an ounce of guts you'll meet me in the parking lot after school today.*

If you got an ounce of guts. Which you don't.

Bontine

When I turned my head around to look at him, he stuck his middle finger up the right side of his nose.

It bothered me all day, of course. I thought Bontine liked Marian Calvert, the girl I had been walking home, but who knows? He was just a belligerent little twit with a chip on his shoulder. His hair looked like a haystack.

People talked about it.

"I hope Bontine beats the hell outta you, Wheeler," said Max Swenson in the hall. That was at noon.

"So, what's it to you, Max?" I said, but he was already off down the corridor with a couple of girls. They were giggling. He was a big basketball shooter, a forward on the Ridgeline team, and I had talked to him maybe once before.

Tammy Hensley walked by with a ring I had sold to a guy named Bennie Flanders about six weeks before. It was hanging from a little gold chain around her neck.

"Hi, Gil," she said. She was a pretty blonde, a little big-boned, with gray eyes. Her hair had a lot of waves in it. She never gave me the time of day either. "I didn't know you liked Marian so much." Then she smiled like Elvis had just squeezed her buns.

I tried to find Marian after lunch but she was nowhere to be seen.

This nervous guy I knew named Steve French came up to me in history class. "I'll go out there with you, man," he said. He stood there leaning back and forth, and his eyes flitted from side to side.

Steve wasn't really the type for fistfights. He was too shy, and he was particularly studious. It was true that he always wanted to do the right thing, but he had no confidence in himself even though he was a very big guy.

"Well, thanks, Steve," I said, "but you don't have to."

"I'll watch your books or something, Gil," he said, blinking his eyes.

"They're not after you," I said. "Jimmy said he's coming."

That was Jimmy Fitch, my pal who loved go-karts, the smallest guy in the eighth grade. Steve was probably the tallest. He was five-eleven or six feet, and all nerves.

"Okay," I said. "Thanks."

The parking lot that afternoon had ten or fifteen guys in it, all acting tough, strutting around. Easy enough for them to do: they didn't have to get their lights punched out.

It was cold and gray, about to snow. You could see your breath.

When I showed up, Bontine started in with a bunch of insults and threats, showing off. Like that jerk Swenson with those girls in the hall. "You ain't walkin' Marian home anymore," he said.

Jimmy just stood there right next to me, a tough little kid if ever there was one, and I handed him my glasses.

One of Bontine's friends named Oliver, a smelly eighth-grader in a motorcycle jacket, walked over to Steve and put his finger on Steve's chest. "You're next, asshole," he said. This guy barely came up to Steve's shoulder, but he was too much for Steve, who was gone in a second. Richard swung at me, and I ducked. But then I started to pummel him. He hit me back pretty hard. After that it was just the usual grunting and swearing and tussling, with whacks in between. I tore a hole in another one of my shirts, or Richard did, and Richard's chin tore open when I shoved his head down into the gravelly dirt.

It went on for maybe three or four minutes, till we were both winded.

We got up off the ground.

Bontine bent over with his hands on his knees, trying to catch his breath, but I stood up. "Enough?"

"Yeah, enough," he said.

"Teacher," said one of his pals.

Jimmy handed me my glasses and we all started walking south toward the corner of the schoolyard and Half Moon Street. Running, really. The tough guys scattered like birds off a wire.

We ran for a while and then slowed down. Bontine wiped his mouth and looked at me and we shook hands.

This sort of stuff, by the way, is never like the movies. You miss most of your punches, you're out of gas real fast, and you get hurt pretty bad. But it only smarts afterwards. Mostly.

To tell you the truth, I kind of felt bad about bashing up Bontine's face, too.

Jimmy pointed back at the school and said, "Look." A high-school guy I knew—Banger Jardine—was leaning back against his Ducati off the side of the road above the parking lot. He was smoking.

"He watched the whole thing," said Jimmy.

"Yeah. I saw him," I said. I told Jimmy who he was. "You know Sonny, my cousin?"

"Yeah."

"They go to Sandia High together."

Banger pumped the starter pedal of his little Bronco. Beautiful sound.

"Do they really call him that?" said Jimmy.

Banger looked almost twenty. He was tall, he had a sharp nose and very close-set eyes, and his hair was slicked back.

I was rubbing my elbow, which was bleeding through my shirt. "Well, his real name is Clarence."

"Wow," said Jimmy.

Banger flipped a butt into the gutter, gunned his engine, and drove off east through one of the side streets toward Eubank Boulevard.

"I'll take a raspberry," said Marian. I was buying her a sno-cone.

"I'll have a cherry cone, please," I said.

The soda shop we were in was next to Griffin's IGA Store off Candelaria Road, and if you weren't nice to the proprietress she would let you know. Her name was Juanita Crosby. *Mrs.* Juanita Crosby.

"That's fifty cents," she said. "Nothing over a five."

She meant that you couldn't pay her with a ten or a twenty. Not that I had one.

She stood there, not moving, staring at me.

I gave her a dollar bill. She took it and dug around in the pocket of her apron. "Here you are, young man," she said. She gave me back five dimes.

I left two on the counter, hoping to appease the dragon, and Marian and I went over to a booth against the wall.

Marian crunched away on her ice. Her blue eyes just sparkled. "She never smiles," said Marian. "Mrs. Crosby."

"She's just a serious person," I said.

"And she loads those dispensers of hers and the ice machine in her trunk and drives around selling sno-cones in the summer. In her Chevy."

"I know. I've bought 'em from her."

Marian smiled at me and shook her paper cone to settle the ice. "You bought me one last August."

"I remember."

Mrs. Crosby was polishing her counter. She worked a damp cloth with the tips of her fingers.

"You want another one, Marian?" I said.

"No," said Marian. "I don't have time." She looked at me sideways. "I'm meeting someone."

"Well, I have to go to work myself."

"You don't own me, you know," she said, chewing the ice.

Own her? I was lucky to see her once or twice a week. And she lived just down the block from me.

"No one owns me," she said, slurping the ice this time. She was fingering a little silver necklace around her throat. "Do you see a ring on this chain?"

"No. Of course not."

"Well, I rest my case." She twirled the chain a little more. "I'm not going steady. With you or anyone."

Now her sno-cone was melting and she tilted it up to sip the raspberry slush.

"That's what I said to Richard, too. His chin looks terrible."

Marian was a charter member of the National Two-Timers' Association. In fact, an original inductee into their hall of fame.

But she was like a flower to me. That's how I thought of her. Maybe a tall purple iris in the spring, unfolding, or a bright orange poppy in the summer. I thought she was luscious, and she smelled very good. She could really kiss you, too. Soft soft soft, everywhere.

But she didn't act like a flower. Flowers don't behold themselves. She was stuck up about her looks. I know she stood in front of the full-length mirror in the hall at her house with something skimpy on when nobody was around just so she could dig herself. Maybe with nothing on. "That's how I work on my posture," she said.

I just tried to ignore this stuff.

Now she was practicing her far-away and wistful look for effect, glancing out the window.

"Hey, Francine," she said. Three or four of her friends came in and went to the counter. Francine Lerner, Steve French's girlfriend, was one of them. "Hi, Marian," she said.

Mrs. Crosby stopped her polishing and perked up a little as the girls ordered.

"You done?" I said.

Marian looked at her watch. "I have five minutes." She put her hand on my arm. "Can I see your elbow?"

"No," I said.

"You and your friends are so immature," she said. She pulled her fingers back. "The high school guys just aren't like that. And your friend Steve?"

She was like a flower to me, but she didn't act like a flower

"What about him?"

"Francine thinks he's a chicken," she said. "Ran from a fight the other day."

"He wasn't involved with that," I said. "He was just a bystander."

"That's not what I heard," she said. "Francine's re-evaluating. Maybe she won't go out with him anymore."

One of Francine's friends put a couple of quarters into Mrs. Crosby's jukebox. So long, Love, sang the Everly Brothers, or words to that effect. So long to your sweet touch.

Marian brushed back a couple of her blonde curls and we went out the door.

"Wait," I said. "I left a notebook." I went back in to get it, and when I came out Marian was already down on the corner of Altez Street and Candelaria. Banger Jardine had pulled his Ducati into the grocery store parking lot, and Marian jumped on the back and they were gone. Just like that.

"Look, man," I heard this voice say. "I'm sorry." The voice was behind me.

I was popping the cords around a bundle of papers down at the shopping center. I looked around. "It's okay, Steve," I said.

I put a dozen of the papers in a little stack beside the door of the gift shop where I usually left them and stuffed the rest into the front and back pouches of my canvas paperbag. Then I left a can on top of the papers for the coins and weighted them down with a little horseshoe I had picked up out in the woods.

"I gotta go, Steve," I said.

He followed me down the sidewalk toward the shoe repair shop.

"I don't know what came over me the other day."

I put down some more papers and another can outside the shoe shop.

"What do I do about that Oliver guy?"

I stopped to turn up my collar against the wind off the mountains to the east. "I can't tell you, Steve. Don't worry about him."

Steve was such a tall guy, lanky but stronger than any one of those fellows in the parking lot by the school. Or me. Or anybody else I knew. And he never saw himself that way.

"I never go looking for any kind of scrap," he said.

"Nobody looks for scraps. They usually just find you."

"Francine thinks I'm a chicken."

I had had about enough of this. "Look, Steve," I said. "I have to go."

"Where?"

I pulled up the paperbags around my shoulders. "Out there," I said. I pointed to the traffic islands over on Menaul Boulevard. "That's where I make my money. It's my job."

His nervous eyes looked up and down Menaul.

"Okay, then," he said.

You would have thought the miscreants were going to get him right there.

"Okay."

"See you later," he said.

"Fight him or don't fight him."

He nodded and went off to the east, back toward his house on Fairbanks Street in Huttontown.

Along Half Moon Street this spotty parade of kids walked toward school. The morning clouds were gray and yellow, flitting by along the top of the sky from the northwest.

Very fast. But down on the ground it was just a little breezy. Pretty chilly.

A guy peeled away from a group of three or four fellows walking half a block in front of me and started back in my direction. It was Bontine.

Damn, I thought. *Here it comes.*

But he just asked me about an assignment we had in speech.

"Not till next week," I said.

"That's good," he said.

"How's your chin?"

"It's okay. How's your elbow?"

"Not bad," I said.

He walked back toward his friends.

"This is it, Steve," said a voice behind me. "No dance next week, no parties, no lunch. Don't call me."

Francine brushed by me on the sidewalk.

Steve came up fast, too. "Francine," he said.

"No, " she said. She was shouting, and Bontine and his friends turned around to look. Steve slipped about two paces behind me.

"That's Oliver up there with Bontine," he said.

Oliver had sticky brown hair caked down behind his ears. He sat in back of Steve in history, too close to pass the sniff test. Francine sat across the aisle from Steve, to his right, and she wouldn't look at him. She was staring from the papers on her desk to the blackboard and back again. Back and forth.

I sat a couple of rows away.

Mr. Holcomb had been lecturing for about ten minutes when Oliver carefully cocked his middle fingers against the pads of his thumbs and popped both of Steve's ears.

Steve dropped his pen.

About five minutes later, Oliver did it again. Steve turned his head and said, "Knock it off." Under his breath. His face was red.

Mr. Holcomb was writing a long list of dates on the board, looking them up and down, and when Oliver flicked Steve's ears for the third time, Steve just kept his eyes straight ahead, doubled up his fist, and swung his right arm around in a reverse haymaker.

Oliver went over backwards and his desk hit the floor along with his head and books.

It was a pretty fair crash.

Mr. Holcomb looked at French and said, "Steve?"

Steve was still flushed. "Yes, sir?"

"Maybe you'd better explain yourself to Mr. Greene." That was the principal.

Oliver was still on the floor. His mouth was a mess.

"Help him up," said Mr. Holcomb.

"Yes, sir," said Steve.

And Francine, who had been looking so carefully at the board, glanced at Oliver and then at Steve and her eyes were like saucers.

Oliver dabbed at his lip with a wad of Kleenexes that Mr. Holcomb gave him and Steve went off down the hall to see Mr. Greene.

Same parade on Half Moon Street, but going south this time in the late afternoon. Mostly kids on foot in twos and threes with all their books and notebooks under their arms or held at their sides. My friend Harold Claus went by on his Eagle with his girlfriend Linda Luchetti on the back. They both waved. Ned Tilman went past on his brother's Triumph. Then Banger drove by on his Ducati with Marian on the pillion. He made a pretty good roar because he had taken the baffles out of his muffler and he was really winding up each gear before he shifted. Marian must have been impressed because she hung on to him with both arms and she gave him a pretty good squeeze as they came up parallel to me.

But she looked the other way.

"Hey, Gil," said this voice. Steve French caught up to me on the sidewalk.

"How are you, Steve?" I said.

"Great," he said. I think he meant it. He was grinning from ear to ear. "Mr. Greene said I was in danger of becoming a menace."

"He didn't haul out his paddle?"

"Not this time. But he warned me. He said I might be a menace. Me. Where are you off to?"

"Just work."

"I don't know what got into me," he said.

"You didn't do anything. You're just a kid trying to take notes in class."

"Francine told me I was a bully," said Steve, "'cause Oliver's half my size."

"Oliver can cram it," I said. "At least he won't bother you anymore."

"Well, at least she's speaking to me again."

I couldn't believe he said that.

Francine went by on the back of a red Jawa. This guy named Dwayne Rowan was the driver. She had both her arms around him, up under his motorcycle jacket. Her red hair was flying out behind her and she stared at Steve for what seemed like minutes as Dwayne headed south.

Steve stared back at her as she disappeared down the block.

"Jesus," he said. "She didn't even wave."

V

The Wizard of Huttontown

"Sad day," I yelled. "Sad day."

It seemed that Mr. Hutton, Burt Hutton, the contractor who had given his name to Huttontown, was gone.

Possibly by his own hand, the paper said.

My friends and I mostly lived in Huttontown. It was more or less our native suburb.

I held up the front page and the headlines must have been three inches high. HUTTON DIES, the paper said.

People gobbled up the papers like popcorn that day, and I sold out in forty-five minutes. Mostly from the auto trade on Wyoming and Menaul, where I walked back and forth on the grimy medians.

I crossed over to the Cosden station, on the other side of Menaul, put a dime in the payphone, and called Mrs. King, my district manager.

"Okay, Gil, I'll see you in twenty or thirty minutes," she said.

When she came she gave me thirty more papers.

I sold those, too, and went back to Huttontown Center, where I had papers in a couple of piles in front of the stores. I walked up and down the sidewalk selling them to people who came to the shops, and I must say they were pretty stunned.

"Can't be," said one guy. He looked like a lawyer. White shirt, nicely pressed; deep blue tie. Creased wool pants. His shirt had French cuffs with blue studs in them. "I just bought a house from him on Parsifal Street three months ago." He gave me a fifty cent tip.

A pretty blonde in a green skirt stopped and pulled a paper out of my hand as she was going into a stationery store. Slowly. "Here," she said, giving me a quarter. She read the headline and a paragraph or two. "Oh, God." She leaned against the door frame.

"Here's your change, ma'am," I said, but she waved me away. Then she turned around, got into her Ford (it was a '54 hardtop, with rattling windows) and drove off up Menaul to the east.

Mr. Hutton's name was everyplace, so I knew he was a great man. Huttontown Shopping Center, said the big sign on the arch right over my head.

Huttontown Baptist Church.

Huttontown Body Shop.

I felt sorry for him because I knew death could be a pitiful thing. I had seen a few people die and sometimes they sobbed as they went, or their friends and relatives did. But I was grateful to him, too, because I had just sold a small mountain of papers. And he had built our house.

One thing Mr. Hutton had going for him was an obvious ability to dream up something and then get it done. You could be a carpenter or a bricklayer and build a house or two every other month and do just fine in the construction business. I had uncles who were in it. There was plenty of money in that to support a family and a car and a trip anytime you wanted to the Pink Elephant, which was the bar a mile and a half west on Menaul. But Hutton built a whole fleet of houses on the open, dry grassland on the east end of Albuquerque, dozens every month, for years, and he did it not just in Huttontown but in the Pines Addition and in other brick subdivisions miles away near the State Fairgrounds. He organized his crews to fill up block after block, one house after another, laid out streets and a shopping center and the beginnings of parks, and fiddled with the bankers and the realtors and the insurance guys to keep it all going.

The city even built schools and wide roads to catch up with him ... *as a result of this beehive of activity and initiative,* the paper said.

So Mr. Hutton was something more than a mason or a framer. We all knew that.

"Sad day," I yelled again. "Sad day."

I sold the last of my newspapers and threw my empty canvas carrier over my left shoulder and began to walk up Claremont Avenue toward my house. After a couple of blocks, I spotted a yellow Chevy panel truck with KQEO 920 AM painted on its back door and both sides. It was sitting at the curb with a little crowd around it.

Ted Nichols, the news guy from KQEO, was doing "man in the street" interviews as I came up. Another very famous man.

"It's your new neighborhood," said Ted, pretty loudly, "and Burt Hutton created it."

"New *suburb,*" said a guy holding back a square-headed dog on a leash.

"Suburb, then," said Ted. "How do you feel?"

"Kind of shocked," said a woman in a house dress with her hair wrapped in a towel. "He was personable, you know."

"He made some money, I suppose," said the guy with the dog. "Now look what good it'll do him." He left his mouth open as he looked around.

My friend Jill Summers was standing on the sidewalk listening to this. Her brother Billy was sitting on his bike just in front of Ted's car.

"How about you, young lady?" Ted started talking to Jill. He looked like Robert Ruark, the newspaper columnist. A dapper guy with a moustache.

"We met him once," said Jill. "Just one time. I'm sorry he had so many troubles. Too many, I guess."

Jill slipped away from the microphone and came over to see me on the sidewalk.

"Did you hear about this, Gil?" she said.

"Yeah. It's the headline this evening in the paper."

"Walk me home," she said.

We both thought we should be somber because of the bad news, but I was happy to see her. She was smiling, too. She lived only a block east and a little south on Fairbanks Street.

"Hi, Gil," said Mrs. Summers. "Can you stay for dinner?" Mrs. Summers pursed her lips and the corners of her mouth turned down a little, but her eyes sparkled.

I put down my newspaper bags on the front porch. "My hands are dirty, Mrs. Summers," I said.

"Wash 'em here at the sink," said Jill, calling over her shoulder to me. We sat down at the table in the kitchen, and she pulled a couple of glasses out of the cupboard and poured us some iced tea. Mrs. Summers picked some mint from a little bed just outside the kitchen door, rinsed it, and gave it to us on a damp towel. We put it in the tea.

"Thanks," I said. "I was pretty dry."

"You work every day, don't you?" said Mrs. Summers.

"Most days," I said.

"KQEO was talking to people down on Claremont," said Jill. "Ted Nichols. He talked to me."

"I was listening to the radio but I didn't hear that. I wish Billy would think about a job," said Mrs. Summers. "Maybe on Saturdays." She was talking mostly to herself. Then she looked at Jill. "What did you say to him?"

"I said Mr. Hutton must have had a lot of troubles."

"That Ted Nichols lives out here. Just across Wyoming on Vermont Street. More tea, Gil?"

"Thanks. This is plenty. My mom will have supper ready."

"But, Jill," said Mrs. Summers, "you're right, of course. That poor man—Mr. Hutton. That's a pity. He seemed happy."

"Bye, Jill," I said. I stood up and chugged down the iced tea. "Thanks again for the drink, ma'am."

Mrs. Summers had the radio on in the kitchen and you could hear Nichols interviewing other people back down on Claremont Avenue or somewhere else in Huttontown.

"You're welcome, Gil," she said. "I'd listen more to that Ted Nichols if his station weren't so awful."

"Mom," said Jill, "it's just Top Forty stuff. We like it."

"Way too loud," Mrs. Summers said. "Too much bass. That Ricky Nelson curls his lip when he sings." She turned back to her stove. "I know you kids like it. At those hops."

Jill smiled at me again. The front door slammed and Billy walked into the kitchen. "That radio guy caught a couple of people crying on the microphone during his interviews. They were all choked up," Billy said, "talking about Mr. Hutton." He started eating pickles and carrots off a little relish tray on the table.

"So long," I said. "Thank you." I edged toward the door.

"You never know," said Mrs. Summers, wiping her fingers on her apron, "what is going on in someone's life. You get a peek or two from the outside, don't you, but you don't see much. Take care, Gil," she said, and she put her hand on my shoulder. After a few seconds she said, "Of course, we usually don't want to look too deeply. We're afraid we'll have to do something with what we find." She was mostly talking to herself.

"Smells like meatloaf," said Billy. He had a new interest in the stove.

It did, more or less, but it was actually chicken Parmesan. I was hungry, but I waved and went back out toward the street.

Mr. Hutton's demise fell like twilight on all the houses in Huttontown. He had made a point of introducing himself and smiling when buyers showed up at his sales office to have a look around the models, and his enthusiasm for his handiwork and the subdivision's location, with the giant wall of the Sandia Mountains behind it, made a strong impression. People bought his brick and block houses by the dozens. Then by the hundreds. They all came in to see him with a lot of Postwar Optimism, as my dad called it, and Hutton's death cut a broad swath right through it.

"He was a founder," said Leo Salisbury, who was somehow an authority on this sort of thing. "Like William Penn or Lord Baltimore back east. Or Don Juan de Oñate out here. Hutton founded this suburb."

Mario Arenas and Tommy Newton and I listened to this in Leo's chaotic bedroom, where he was showing us the power of a big magnet he had just bought at Van's Bicycles and Hobbies. It was a shop just across Menaul from the Huttontown Shopping Center. Salisbury had science fiction books and sprawling gadgetry falling out of a series of floor-to-ceiling metal shelves shoved against the walls around the bed.

He went into his garage and came back with a steel card table in one hand and a quart Miracle Whip jar full of iron grains in the other. We used to go on expeditions to pull the black iron bits out of the sand in the arroyo bottoms north and east of town with our lodestones, which were plenty strong, but Leo had the heaviest magnet we had ever seen.

"It's off a generator," he said. He was grinning.

"How much?" said Mario.

"Only a couple of bucks."

Leo's friend Tommy was staring at him.

"Well, three-fifty," said Leo.

The magnet hung upside down under the center of the steel table and Leo shook some grains out of the jar into his hand. He cast the iron bits onto the tabletop with a sweeping motion and a magical pattern of lines appeared. It looked like the two ears of a goblin set close together.

"The magnetic field," said Leo, all showman with his new baritone voice. He stuck his hand under the table, pulled the magnet sideways, and distorted the ears. The tabletop sagged in the middle under the weight of the thing.

"My dad used to work for him," said Mario. "He was one of his framers."

"Hutton?" I said.

"Yeah. The guy who died."

"I knew a guy who painted trim for him," said Newton. He was standing near an open window in Leo's room, smoking cigarettes.

"How is this guy any different than these other guys out there?" said Mario. "You know—in the Heights? Like Ed Snow and Coda Roberson. Or Mossman. They've built a lot of new subdivisions, too." Their names were plastered all over billboards that we saw all the time.

"My old man was friends with Bellamah," I said. "He built Princess Jeanne Park. They were at the university together."

"Well, none of them built a shopping center," said Leo, "except Hutton. It's fundamental."

We all nodded at this bit of sagacity while the sage spilled a new batch of iron grains on the floor. He nudged the table as he bent over to gather them up. One of its legs folded, and the magnet hit the floor with a bang and gouged a chunk out of the linoleum.

"Hell," said Leo.

Mario said, "Maybe we should do something for him. I mean, that's pretty bad, dying like that."

"What do you have in mind?" I said.

"We planted a tree for my granddad," said Mario. "He died in Silver City and the nuns let us put it on their school ground. Out in front, where the grass was."

"Was it some kind of park?" said Leo.

"Yeah," said Mario. "Pretty much. Up Bear Mountain Road down there."

"There's no park out here," said Tommy.

"They're fundamental," said Leo, "and yes, there is that open space down between Phoenix and Fairbanks streets. It's gonna be a park. Hutton Park, actually."

"Fundamental to what?" I said.

"A suburb, of course," said Leo.

"Actually, we could use a restaurant out here, you know," said Newton. "Or a café or something."

"Leo," said a woman's voice down the hall. Leo's mom. "Leo, are you smoking? And what was that thump?"

"Dammit, Tommy," said Leo.

"Oh, Jesus," said Newton. He stubbed out his cigarette and threw it out the window.

"No, Mom," said Leo. "No problem."

Mario, who was a short, stocky kid with dark brown hair, sat down on the edge of Leo's bed. "Well, we could get a little tree at that nursery on Menaul by Pennsylvania Street and plant it somewhere."

"Not bad," said Leo. "But where?"

"Above the Whitewash," I said. "Up at the end of Menaul. There's water up there and it would grow. Besides, it looks out over the city."

We all chipped in and bought a little one-gallon limber pine for four bucks at the nursery the next Saturday morning and took it back to Salisbury's house, but Newton would have nothing to do with it.

"What the hell do I care?" he said. "Dale Bellamah built everything on my street." He lived somewhere over near Jackson Junior High, east of Eubank Boulevard. Close to Snow Heights. Technically he was right, of course. He didn't live in Huttontown. But he was also cheap and never paid for anything.

"Your suburb is incomplete, Tommy," said Salisbury. "It's just houses with an arroyo ripping through."

Mario had borrowed a black '57 Cushman Eagle from one of his friends, and Salisbury had somehow gotten hold of a green Triumph Tiger Cub from this high school guy named Gene McNally who lived just down the street. It was a coup. That was the most beautiful machine in

We all chipped in and bought a little one-gallon limber pine

Huttontown and it just hummed a nice English tune when Gene drove it up and down and around the block. His mother doted on him and always kept him tucked under her wing. So we never saw him go much further than that, and as a result the Triumph was in mint condition.

"He owes me a favor," said Leo.

I tucked the pine into my canvas knapsack, put in a canteen, a little GI shovel, and a box of Wheat Thins, slung the thing over my shoulder, and climbed on the tiny pillion behind Mario. He revved the accelerator and crunched the gearshift into first and killed the engine.

"Jesus Christ, kid," said Leo, looking across at us from the Triumph, which purred beautifully. "Don't drive much, do you?"

Mario and I got off and he tilted up the starter pedal with his toe. Then he bounced up into the air and with the pad of his right foot pushed the starter pedal down to the floor plate. He cranked the handgrip throttle around hard and the engine caught right away.

Leo led east on Menaul and we soon ran out of pavement. We drove along the dirt track with our legs out and kicked the ground quite a bit when we crossed arroyos to keep from spinning out and falling. The wheels on the Tiger Cub were a lot larger, of course, so Leo didn't slip in the decomposed granite as much as Mario and I did and he went faster than we could manage. He was already at the base of the Whitewash, parking the Triumph in the shade of a boulder, as we drove up.

"Up there, Gil?" he said, pointing to the top of the enormous granite outcrop. They had told us in class once that it was a Precambrian relic, a billion or more years old, stuffed into the mouth of its canyon. A trickle of clear water plunged down the face of it just left of center. You could see it easily from Huttontown, miles away.

We passed around the Wheat Thins for fortification. Then we locked the motors up with chains to a convenient but very sticky piñon. Leo adjusted the straps of his own small rucksack and I moved mine off to one shoulder.

"How about up here?" said Mario. He was calling down to us from the top of the Whitewash.

When Salisbury and I got up there, we saw that he had found a little sandy bench covered with Apache plume and bricklebrush at the edge of the tiny stream that trickled along toward its plunge off the rim of that granite cliff. The bench looked west out of the canyon with a clear view of the long string of cottonwoods marking the Rio Grande and of Vulcan and Jo, the tent-top volcanoes beyond. You could see Mount Taylor in the blue distance seventy miles beyond that.

"Gil?" said Leo.

"Sure," I said. I put my knapsack down. "Looks like the right spot."

It only took a minute or so to dig a hole for the tiny tree in the wet beach sand. We got the pine out of its pot and into the ground and mulched it up nicely with leaf litter. Then we scooped up water from the creek with our hands and soaked it.

Salisbury pulled a section of the morning paper out of his knapsack and flipped through it as we all stood there looking at the Rio Grande valley.

"He was the 'Wizard of Huttontown'," said Salisbury. That's what one of his friends said." He was reading from the Obits page. *Burt Hutton did what he did better than any other developer in post-war Albuquerque. Or New Mexico, for that matter.*

We tossed stones over the lip of the massive rock and watched them tumble down to the bottom.

"My old man liked him," said Mario. "Said he always paid on time."

"What about your old man, Gil?" said Salisbury.

But before I could answer, he said, "My dad grimaced when he heard about Mr. Hutton. 'The trees are just startin' to put on a little height out here,' he said, 'around Hutton's new houses.'"

"Well, here's another one for him," said Mario. He cupped his hands together and bent over and drank out of the little stream. "If it grows."

VI

Jack Sutton

JACK WAS TAKING NOTES, sitting quietly in an eighth grade history class, but it made no difference. These two guys, one of them fat in a gray suit and the other one skinny and weaselly with short sleeves and a string tie, came in and talked to Mr. Holcomb, the teacher, who was in the middle of a speech on the Carthaginians, and then just walked over and grabbed Jack. No ceremony or decorum about it.

They took him off down the hall. To the D-Home, or Springer, the State Delinquent Boys' School.

You could hear Jack clear across the school. Everybody but the kids in the gym or out on the bike and motorcycle parking lot heard him.

"Mary Ann," he yelled. "Mary Ann!"

Jack was crying and kicking the two guys. They were a lot bigger than he was, of course, and they just lifted him up by the elbows and hauled him down the corridor.

He kept yelling for Mary Ann Nickerson, and when she finally heard him they had him out the front door and

71

were carrying him toward a white state car all covered with mud from the January rains.

"Shut up," said the fat guy in the gray suit. He slapped Jack with the back of his hand. The other guy—the weasel—lost his grip on Jack's elbow and dropped him to the ground.

Jack lay there all curled up in a ball and crying. It was muddy. He was kicking with one leg and pushing himself around in a tight little circle. You could see his breath in the air as he panted.

Mary Ann Nickerson came up and she was crying, too. A couple of her pals followed her—Nancy Hartman, I think, and Sharon Townes—girls like Mary Ann in petticoat skirts, and Mrs. Crook the English and Latin teacher was fussing with Mary Ann, trying to get her to come back to the school building. But she just dropped down and spread herself across Jack and cried and dared the two state guys to touch her. She hugged Jack and wailed. She was all worked up.

It didn't do much good.

All the kids on the south side of the main Ridgeline building had gone to the windows.

The principal, Mr. Greene, came up and shouted at the two guys. "My school," he said. "You come through my office."

They shouted back at him to lay off. "This is state business," said the fat guy. A couple of the football jocks in Jack's class bet each other that Jack would run then, but he didn't.

Mrs. Crook took Mary Ann by the arm and inched her back toward the front entrance. The junior high girls sometimes wore these long skirts with a lot of can-can petticoats under them and the skirts bounced back and forth, rocking like a short swing with no one in it. Mary

*The two guys drove off with Jack down Half Moon Street
to the south and disappeared*

Ann's dark green skirt looked like it would swing up and hit her on the chin when she moved. She was shaking. Nancy and Sharon were crying. Even Mrs. Crook, who was crusty—believe me—was dabbing her eyes.

The weasel picked Jack up by the arms and the gray suit got him by the legs and they lugged him off screaming to the car.

We had a good opinion of Mr. Greene, the principal. He was a pretty fair man. He stood there trying to figure out what to do. He yelled at the state guys again. He walked around to the back of the car and took down the license number. It was a government plate. Then he turned on his heels and trotted back toward his office.

"I'll bet he's gonna call somebody," said my friend Jimmy Fitch.

I think he did call, but nothing happened. It made no difference.

The two guys drove off with Jack down Half Moon Street to the south and disappeared.

All this took place under a cold china-blue sky in January, as clear and sparkling a day as there ever was in New Mexico, with spidery clouds over the south horizon, very high, edging across the sky on their way to the mountains.

There was a party about a week later at Dave Casey's house off Eubank Boulevard and I took Mary Ann. Her dad dropped us off. She had a long blonde ponytail and a spit curl on her forehead and pale green eyes and she was maybe an inch or two taller than I was. I hadn't grown much yet. But I had hopes, and my voice was deepening a bit. I was wishing she'd notice.

No matter. We were dancing to "La Bamba" and "Oh, Donna" by Ritchie Valens and to a couple of Champs 45s and drinking some kind of punch.

Casey, the sort of guy who was everyone's friend, had a cute girlfriend named Sherry. Big dimples on both sides of her mouth. She was from Clovis or Lovington or some other semi-Texan town on the east side of New Mexico. She thought Dave was pretty exotic because his family was French Canadian and they often put their heads together and made plans or cracked jokes and gave each other advice and directions in French. His mom and his sister were doing just that over in the corner of the front room.

"Dave, it's like being in Paris or Marseilles or somewhere," said Sherry. "You are so cool. What are they saying now?"

Casey grinned. "Ma petite mègére," he said.

"Oh Dave," she said.

"My little fox," he said.

Sherry was hanging onto him like Saran Wrap.

What a phenomenal technique for a guy who otherwise was just an amiable kid in junior high. You had to give it to him.

Dave and Sherry and Mary Ann and I started to play Spin the Bottle in Dave's bedroom and I got so excited the bottle slipped through my fingers. So Mary Ann spun it and somehow it actually slowed down and pointed at me and we stood up and stepped into the closet.

It smelled like tweed cloth and a little like mothballs in there. A tiny blue light was stuck into a socket in one corner. She kissed me after we fumbled around a bit and I kissed her back and her mouth was amazingly wet. She pressed up against me and she had her fingers in my hair.

Then she put her little finger inside the whorls of my right ear. Very lightly.

She pulled back a little, embarrassed. But then she smiled and kissed me again, on the cheek this time. She smelled like wisteria flowers.

This stuff made your head spin. We were both out of breath.

As we stepped out of the closet we looked away from each other, but I could see she was flushed.

We liked to think we were pretty big kids, of course, but maybe we weren't so big.

As I walked her home from Casey's I wanted to kiss her again, but it was too cold. You had to keep moving. We had about a mile and a half to go. We walked down the frozen streets with our hands in our pockets and the frost crackled on the ground. The stars were out and we both had on jackets that were too light.

At Hutton Park we walked under the leafless tree crowns spread out against the sky. Their limbs were white in the moonlight. We stopped for a minute and sat on a wooden bench to look at the moon.

"Put your arm around me, Gil," she said. She snuggled up next to my ribs. Then she said, "Jack's just my friend."

"I heard you were just friends."

"Our families are friends. He drinks."

"That what got him into trouble?"

"More than that," she said. "He's got a crowbar, and he goes around at night."

One more of those kisses. Boy, could she kiss. But her lips were cold this time, and she was shivering.

"Let's go," she said.

As we were walking she let me hold her hand for the last block or so, and we were right on the money. Right on time. I said good night to her at the stroke of ten and her mom actually smiled at me at the door.

That cold weather lasted. It warmed up a little several weeks later, in March, but the spring wind was blowing by then and it was still pretty chilly.

I thought about Jack sometimes, and all his troubles. Mary Ann wouldn't say anything more about him.

I tried hard to avoid scuffles after school and on the weekends, and did pretty well for a few weeks. But this kid named Bobby Hiller, the kind of guy who would press you endlessly, pushed all my buttons one day and I punched him out in the schoolyard.

My history teacher, Mr. Holcomb, caught the two of us in the middle of that messy business and marched us back toward the main building. When we got to the school he pushed us down the hall to the office. Mr. Greene made us cool our heels on a row of chairs set against a wall in the reception room before he talked to us.

I could see through the low windows straight down the hall due east of the school office. Jack had been dragged down that corridor maybe six weeks earlier. School wasn't due to start for another ten minutes and I knew Mary Ann's locker was just down the hall and around the corner. I kept looking for her.

I had a generally good reputation in that school, or so I thought, but Mr. Greene had a poor opinion of fights and a wide flat paddle to back up his opinion.

I had busted Hiller's lip but he had opened up a little strip under my right eye and he and I sat there dabbing at the wounds with our handkerchiefs.

The principal was talking to Mr. Holcomb behind his closed door and their voices sounded even and low. When he opened the door and motioned us in I saw the paddle laid out carefully on his blotter with the handle hanging off the right side of his desk. There was a hole bored in the small end and a cord dangled from it. Mr. Holcomb came up to us, pointed toward Mr. Greene, and said, "Move quietly."

I did it, but I was looking back over my shoulder and I saw Mary Ann and her friend Nancy Hartman coming around the far end of the hall as we went into the office, and the principal made us sit and in a slow smooth motion locked the door.

VII

Through the Woods Like a Pair of Ghosts

"I'D LIKE to be ambidextrous," I said, "and a mountain man."

Mr. Holcomb stopped for a minute. "Mountain man," he said.

"Yes, sir," I said. "Like Kit Carson or Ceran St. Vrain. You could live up in the high Rockies and catch trout with your hands and roast them on a stick over the fire. Find beaver and trap 'em. Sharpen your knife blade on a stone."

Now he nodded at me. "You like the woods then, Gil?"

"Yes, sir," I said. "You can't spend enough time in the mountains."

I had thought that for years. The air smelled good up there and you saw deer and coyotes and sometimes bobcats as you hiked along if you were quiet and steady enough. Blue jays and hawks up in the trees or in the air. Aspens against the blue sky and lanky ponderosa pines that smelled like vanilla.

You could even find all these wonders in the mountains just to the east of us. The Sandias. Well, a lot of them, anyway.

It was mostly benign up there in the Rockies, but sometimes it was dangerous. The weather could turn on you in ten minutes and you would get soaked and freeze. Or you could be off in the brush exploring a canyon somewhere and crack your shinbone or break your foot. The footing was always unsure. You'd never limp out by yourself: the place would just eat you alive, a piece at a time. It didn't suit everyone. For instance, I knew some guys who were afraid to drink out of creeks. Their tongues, of course, would ultimately swell up and they would perish of thirst.

Carson and St. Vrain mastered all these difficulties, toiled ceaselessly to squeeze a living out of all those valleys and peaks, learned to get along with the locals, and came to be so good at what they did that they could slip through the woods like a pair of ghosts. They wove themselves into the forest.

"Ambidextrous?" said Mr. Holcomb.

"Yes, sir—like Leonardo da Vinci and some of the mountain men," I said. "Like Hugh Glass, for instance. I'd like to be able to do things with either hand. Draw or paint. Throw a ball or knife. Maybe shoot a rifle."

"You have a lot of experience with that?" said Mr. Holcomb.

"Not much, no," I said. "Just some."

But I had bought a pair of flat-bladed throwing knives through the mail and was just then mauling the trunk of an elm tree in my backyard with nightly practice. With both hands.

"What the hell are you doing over there?" said Mr. Fields, my next-door neighbor. He was pretty loud.

On a few occasions the blades had missed their mark and zipped over the back wall into his yard. You could hear them clanking across his concrete patio. Left-hand throws, mostly. "Sorry, sir," I said, and I scrambled to get them back.

"I have more experience with fishing," I said to Mr. Holcomb.

Jimmy Fitch raised his hand. "I wanna do something with cars," he said. Jimmy's dad ran a body shop. "Maybe design 'em."

Jimmy could draw nicely, and he was a neatnik. He would take a week to draw a new Corvette or T-Bird and another week to color it in, with nothing out of place, no strokes showing. He usually sketched in flames shooting out behind the front wheel wells.

When Holcomb asked the girls in the class about their future, one of them said, "Maybe teaching." That was Pat Clifton, whose old man owned a bar and lounge downtown. "Maybe I could teach civics in high school," she said.

"And where would you study for that?" said Mr. Holcomb.

"Well, the University of Montana," said Pat. "In Missoula. My mom's college. They're good at civics."

Marian Calvert, my kissing instructor, said, "Biology. I want to work in a lab." She had talked to me once about the University of Denver. "Not just anybody can get in, you know," she said.

Leo Salisbury said, "Engineering. Mechanical, I think."

They were all smart kids, and as I listened to them I thought that my own comments were glaringly based on obsolete sixteenth- or nineteenth-century notions. Probably impractical.

"It's a technical world now," said Mr. Holcomb, "and you'll need to prepare technically for it. You'll have to add science and math to your social studies."

I didn't care. I liked the Renaissance and I liked the idea of the Rocky Mountain fur trade.

To me Mr. Holcomb said, after the bell rang, "What have you been reading?"

"Kit Carson's *Autobiography*," I said. "And a book by an English guy named Clark on Leonardo."

To my surprise, he said, "Keep it up. Try that book on the Taos Trail by Lewis Garrard, or *Lord Grizzly*."

"You might want to be a mountain man, Gil," said Mario, "but I just want to be a guy with a job. I gotta get something."

We were at Leo's house after school. Leo was getting ready to go over to Tommy Newton's place, or Newton's uncle's place, to work on cars. They were finally paying him. He had rebuilt his little Harley Hummer after a lot of tries and he was going to give me a ride to my own job on the way, just to show me how it ran.

"I need the money," said Mario. He never talked like that. "You guys both have jobs. I gotta get up to speed."

"What's eating Arenas?" I said to Salisbury as we rode down to the shopping center. Leo's Harley was very slow, but it purred as we went along.

"His mom lost her job," said Leo over his shoulder. "She got laid off. He's worried about things." We went down Phoenix Avenue along the south side of Hutton Park. The city crews were out planting new elms around the edges. No grass yet, but the trees were a nice touch.

We were between classes a couple of days later when Mario said, "Let's go down to the university. Maybe next week. I think we're off on Wednesday."

"It's illegal," said Leo. "You can't just stroll onto a college campus."

"Why not?" said Mario. "It's a public place."

"Why Wednesday?" I said.

"Because it's a teachers' mental health day," said Mario. "They're all gone to some conference. No school."

"Wow," said Leo.

"We'd have to go early," I said. "In the morning. I've got papers in the afternoon."

"But look," said Leo. "This is a public place, too. This school. But if we walked around here real late in the afternoon or at night we'd get busted."

"I asked my old man," said Mario. "Anybody can visit the university. Even kids."

"I thought you were looking for a job, Mario," I said. "Find one?"

"I got an idea," he said. "I might have some news after next Wednesday."

"Might be fun down there," said Leo. "At the university. We could look around a little."

We had talked about college a lot of times before, in class and out, but really we were completely clueless. It was a mythical place to us.

My cousin Sonny Wheeler, the high school kid, looked at me like I was recently arrived from the planet Mars when I mentioned the university to him. "Pete Kiley's there," he said. Kiley was a year or so ahead of Sonny, and out of high school by then. "You know Pete Kiley?"

Who didn't? He was the most famous morning newspaper mogul in the east end of Albuquerque. He lived with two or three equally cool brothers on the south side of Hutton Park. The brothers threw papers, too, and Pete drove a beautiful '54 Ford, a two-tone, two-door sedan. It was emerald green on the lower body, with a cream-colored roof. Pete had little pulleys set up just behind the rear-view mirror to help him dispense his paper-rolling string. Two-ply, if I remember right. Pretty light. You could snap it off the outside of your little finger with no trouble.

Everyone knew him for speed. He could roll twenty papers a minute on light days, piling them up into a mountain on the back seat, and he had four morning routes. Hundreds of papers. I don't know how he did it. He must have started out about 3:30 a.m. every day, and he was done by six.

He made a small fortune, and it was propelling him through the university.

"Yeah, Sonny, I know Pete Kiley," I said. "I've seen him around." "Around" meant Pete looked over at me from his Ford while he was waiting for the light to change when I was selling papers off the street islands in the afternoon. Cold eyes, I thought. Kind of a cocky guy, but still impressive.

"Well, he's at the university. Majoring in finance," said Sonny. Sonny threw a route in the morning that Pete wanted to gobble up. It was right in the middle of his empire, said Sonny, but as yet indigestible.

I mentioned Pete to Leo and Mario.

"What the hell is 'finance'?" said Mario.

"Part of economics," said Leo. "It's business. Like banking. The guy is a business major."

With Leo you were sure that the Pope and the Secretary of the Treasury briefed him on a daily basis.

The bus driver watched us in his rear-view mirror as he drove down Central Avenue. It was ten in the morning and the only other person on board was a tiny old lady who clutched a big paper sack (and her purse) to herself with both hands.

Central Avenue was Route 66, and we went past motels with big neon signs, a lot of curio shops selling trinkets like the rings I refinished from Mexico and a handful of real pots from the Pueblos, and a few famous cafes like Hoyt's Dinner Bell and Leonard's Restaurant. *Ben-Hur* was playing at the Lobo Fine Arts Theater.

The university came up fast. We pulled the cord to get off at Yale Boulevard, and when we walked by the driver up front, he said, "Two more zones, you guys. That's twenty cents more apiece. Each. Exact change." We gave him some more dimes, got out of there, and walked north.

There was a big stadium with some guys out practicing runs and a three or four story building that said *Geology* over the door on our left. And in the distance the library tower loomed up in the sky. It was a lot taller than anything else. The whole place looked pretty much like Taos Pueblo in a meadow.

"A university is an essential part of a real city," said Leo. "Of course, you'll find nothing like this out where we come from."

"We're essentially lost," said Mario.

Students were walking in all directions, looking serious, trying to make class on time. "They dress up," said Mario, with his head turning from side to side, and it was true. The girls were old, but they were plentiful in their soft sweaters and still gorgeous for their advanced years.

We tried hard not to stand out, but we were like little warthogs in a field of very graceful gazelles.

We wandered through the halls of a new classroom building and peeked through the tiny window panes in the doors at the students taking notes. We tried to make no noise at all. Then we came to a sizable lecture hall with its door propped open.

Prehistory of the Southwest, said a neatly typed card tucked into a bracket on the wall. *MWF, 11:00 – 11:50 a.m. F. C. Hibben, Professor.*

My jaw dropped. It was the guy who discovered Sandia points and the Sandia culture. Early Man in the New World. I had read his book in the Ridgeline library.

We peeked in.

A slide show was going, the students were stupefied, and the professor was pointing to a line of grimy pots on the screen with a little baton.

"Who are you trying to find, boys?" said this voice behind us.

We jumped back away from the door.

The voice belonged to a serious-looking blonde in a pressed white blouse and a greenish wrap-around skirt. "What class are you looking for?"

"We're looking for Lonnie Wilkins's office," said Mario. "Are you the president?"

She laughed. "Maybe someday. No, I'm a graduate student. A graduate assistant." She must have been all of twenty-two.

"May I shake your hand?" said Leo. "I'm Leo Salisbury. I've never met a graduate assistant." He pumped her right hand. "What an honor."

"Where's the Physical Plant?" said Mario. "I've got an appointment at 11:45."

She told us.

"Do you know Pete Kiley?" I said. "I think he's a finance major."

She shook her head. "No, but there are nine thousand undergraduates and graduates here. What are you guys

"We're essentially lost," said Mario

doing out of school?" she said. "It's the middle of the week."

"Well, we're not playing hooky, ma'am," said Mario, "if that's what you're thinking." He looked at the clock on the wall. "Teachers' day off at our school. We'll have to go now."

"What's your major?" said Leo.

"History and anthropology," she said.

"What's your name?" I said. "I'm Gil. Gil Wheeler."

"Carol Shelton," she said. She smiled at us. "Good luck, fellas. Look me up when you get here."

"You can bet on that," said Leo.

Mario came out of his meeting with Mr. Wilkins a half hour later, biting his lip. "He told me I could get on as a junior intern with the HVAC guys this summer," he said.

"Is that heating and cooling?" I said.

"Yeah."

"Wow, Mario—nice going," said Leo.

"Yeah, but it's three months away. I need something now."

There was a guy selling hot dogs out of a cart shaded by a blue umbrella in front of the immense library, so we bought six of them with mustard and relish and three bottles of pop and sat down under some pines to eat. Mario had bummed a buck from me to buy his share, and he said, "I'll pay you back tomorrow, Gil. I got a little stash in a can in my room."

"Next week is okay," I said.

"No, I can do it tomorrow," he said.

"Why don't you try the Debonair Shoe Shop in the shopping center?" I said. "I know that guy. His name is Simpson. He's got a shine chair and I think he's ready to hire somebody. Maybe. You know how to shine shoes?"

"Sure," said Mario.

"Well, try him out. He's not a bad guy."

We finished the dogs and went into the library to look around. We had only read about murals before, and here the place had a bunch of them high on the wall behind the check-out desk. They were figures from the old days in New Mexico, stoic Pueblo people and Spanish farmers and Anglos with big wide eyes. The plaque said they were done by hard-up painters in the Depression maybe twenty years before, and they were underlit, in big niches, with terrific shadows.

About sixty feet away from the check-out desk the building split like a cross into three long reading rooms, with sunlight streaming down from the high windows. The ceilings were forty or fifty feet tall with big beams (Mario said they were called *vigas*) and rows of diagonally-set lath cross-pieces, thin but stout-looking, laid over them.

"Those are the *latillas*," said Mario.

"Shhh," said the librarian. She was stacking books on a counter at another desk behind us.

"Sorry," I said.

We had never been in a building that big, or that beautiful.

It was so still in the place that you could have heard a feather floating down from the ceiling to the floor, and we just stood there for five or ten minutes and took it in.

Leo boned up on his technical reading after our trip to the university and said that he wanted to be an *industrial—* rather than a mechanical—engineer.

Mario talked to Mr. Simpson at the cobbler's shop, laid on some charm that I had never been able to muster, and got hired. I saw him in the afternoons as I was tending my papers, and once I asked him to give me a shine rather than doing it myself at home. He was fast and good. He got Mr. Simpson to put taps on the heels of his shoes, even though it was against the code at Ridgeline, just so he could for once in his life be really cool. He was slight and slightly bow-legged—close to the ground, you might say, and for weeks he made quite a distinct clicking racket as he walked down the halls. I thought he had gotten away with it. But Mr. Postlethwaite, the science guy, finally nabbed him and he had to pull the cleats off with a claw hammer extracted from the janitor's closet while Mr. Science watched.

"Next time it's detention," said Mr. Postlethwaite, "or worse."

I read up on Renaissance mural-making in a book by a guy named Vasari, and Mr. Holcomb gave me a little hardback to look at on a Wyoming mountain man named Jim Bridger. It was ruckus after ruckus in those books with the Crows and Blackfeet in the northern Rockies, and with the Medici and guys like the Duke of Milan in Italy. Unmatched scenery in the one place and the best paintings in the world in the other, you might say, but somebody was always dying.

Turbulent places, both of them.

I asked Pat Clifton, the bartender's daughter, to go to a sock hop in the gym with me. There was something about the way she pursed her mouth when she was daydreaming that got me—beautiful pink lips in a perfect Cupid's bow and her gray eyes. That sort of stuff.

"Nope," she said. "No soap. I'm going with Mike Pickett." That was a tall ninth-grader I knew, another jock.

So that was that.

I was standing in the median a day or so later, hawking papers, and turning my back every five minutes to the nasty west wind. It was full of flying grit that crunched between your teeth.

The light changed to red after one or two wind blasts and I turned around to see Pete Kiley with his left elbow out the window of his Ford, looking at me.

"Can I have a couple of those papers?" he said. "We have a lot of readers in our house."

"Sure," I said. I handed him a pair of crisp ones. "Just back from the university?"

He gave me a fifty-cent piece. "Yeah," he said. "Makes for a long day."

I dug down into my carpenter's apron for change.

"Keep it," he said.

"Thanks. Do you have four routes?" I said, but the wind came up hard again with flying dust and I had to duck my head.

The light changed.

"No," he said. He put the Ford into first. "Just three. But that's enough, I can tell you." He started to pull away. "Three can really take it out of you, you know."

VIII

The Ring Trade

"Are you gonna buy that?" she said.

"Maybe a few of them," I said.

Jill and I were standing in the middle of the big market in Ciudad Juárez, the old one on 16th of September.

"¿En cuánto se vende?" I said to the guy in the booth. *How much?*

"En tres cada uno." *They're three each.*

"Dollars or pesos?" I said.

The guy smiled, but wearily. "It's oro, not plata," he said. *U.S. money, not Mexican.* "I don't like to bargain with kids. No me juegues." *Don't play around with me.*

He put down a cigar.

"¿Se puede en uno y medio?" I said. *How about one-fifty?*

"How many?" he said. "¿Cuántos?"

"Five."

"Pick 'em," he said. "Two bucks."

"Okay," I said.

He wrapped up the five switchblades in a couple of pieces of newspaper and I gave him ten bucks.

"I'm thirsty," said Jill.

We walked down 16th of September to a Sanborn's and went in and I ordered Cokes for both of us. "Sin hielo," I said to the waitress. *No ice.* "Por favor."

"Sure," she said.

"I'm hungry, too," said Jill.

I ordered a couple of bowls of menudo when the waitress came back and she smiled at my careful Spanish. "You sound like a Northerner," she said. She meant a guy from northern New Mexico. "¿Eres?" *Are you?*

"Kind of," I said. "Yeah."

Jill and I were both about fourteen (we liked to think nearly fifteen) and this trip was the first she had ever taken away from the watchful eyes of her parents. It was with kids from her church, but I knew a lot of them.

"What's in this?" she said. She tore off another piece of warm tortilla and lapped up the steaming soup with her big Mexican spoon.

"Don't ask," I said.

"When were you here before?" she said.

"A couple of times. Once when I was a little kid, with my dad."

"The Coke's good, too," she said. "Very icy." I guess the waitress couldn't help herself.

"When you finish, we'll go and get some more stuff," I said. "I've got a few orders."

"Who from?"

"Leo Salisbury and Tommy Newton. A friend of Jimmy Fitch's wanted a bullwhip. Bill Pike. Ray Dailey and Will Carnes wanted rings for their girlfriends. So did Steve French. Jeff Stahl. He doesn't have a girlfriend yet but he's hoping. Or maybe he just likes the rings."

"We've got to get back to the bus in an hour and a half," said Jill.

It was a little cool outside, a late afternoon in mid-October. Not much of a breeze.

We went back to the market and bought some bullwhips. Of all the stuff you could buy in Juárez—and believe me, there was an endless supply of it—the bullwhips were maybe the most useless. But my pals and I had all watched Lash LaRue and Zorro on TV and we knew you would have success with horses and girls if you only popped them right. Preferably ten feet or so behind your shoulder, with a big crack.

The market smelled good from the jicamas and chiles and melons and all the spices that were for sale. The sunlight streamed down into the place from the slot windows in the high roof and spotlighted heaps of produce and merchandise. The cilantro was sharp and fresh, and its tiny leaves glistened from the drops of water that the vendors sprinkled on them.

Jill bought a little velvet painting of an island with palm trees and the sea behind it. "This is really something," she said. "What does it say?" She touched the artist's signature in the lower right-hand corner.

"Acosta," I said. The dealer in the little gallery beamed at her. "My cousin," he said. "He paints these in Hidalgo del Parral."

We found a booth with hundreds of rhodium-coated rings, all tumbled together in a couple of straw baskets. The woman behind the counter was impatient. She shifted her weight from leg to leg and glanced off down the aisles toward the door. She was middle-aged and worried-looking. "Ahorita me voy," she said. *I have to go soon.*

"Forty minutes," said Jill. "We have to meet everyone at the bus."

The big rhodium rings were the kind the high school guys liked to give their girlfriends when they asked them

The rhodium, whatever that was, glistened like silver

to go steady. They were narrow like a wedding band on the underside but they flared out on top to about three-quarters of an inch. I could usually find them at curio stores on Central Avenue in Albuquerque, but they were expensive. The Mexicans glued or sometimes soldered a thick rectangular brass plate on the top part and crowned that with a little rhodium-covered skull or a couple of rhinestones. Maybe some glass rubies or a tiny car. It was pretty impressive, and the rhodium, whatever that was, glistened like silver until it started to wear off. Of course, the doodads on top came loose after you wore one of these things for a few days, and that left bits of brass exposed. If you ground the top down with a little medium and fine sandpaper, and afterward touched that work up with buffing cloth (an old handkerchief would do) and some brass polish, the ring looked pretty good. *Really* good, actually. The brass took on a great shine.

The high school guys might have been impressed with the results. I don't know. But the junior high kids loved those modified rings, and I had a lot of requests for them. I popped the skulls and the fake jewels off with a screwdriver and polished the brass hard. I charged three-fifty each. Sometimes four bucks. To most people.

"How many do you want?" said the lady at the booth. She kept looking at the door and rocking back and forth.

"Maybe ten," I said. *Como diez.*

"Twelve-fifty," she said.

"¿Se puede en diez?" I asked. *How about ten?*

"Okay," she said. "No more talking. Ten for ten. Pick ten."

That was all the cash I had except for my reserve, which was also ten bucks.

I counted out the money and picked out the rings in different sizes.

Jill and I walked fast down the pot-holed sidewalks and got to the Santa Fe Bridge in about fifteen minutes. The Rio Grande dribbled along under the bridge in puddles and filmy lines, and down on the riverbed kids with long poles that had cardboard funnels wired to their ends kept pace with us and pled for change. "Throw us something," they yelled. "Come on: something." We tossed over some quarters.

We got to the bus just beyond the U.S. Customshouse with five minutes to spare.

"What was in that soup we ate?" said Jill. We were back in our seats.

"You liked it, didn't you?"

"Sure. It was as good as I've ever had."

"Tripe," I said. *Tripas.*

"Oh, Jesus," she said.

"Jill," said Mrs. Curtis, her Sunday School teacher, who was sitting three rows behind us. "Jill, don't you blaspheme."

The old hotel on the plaza in El Paso—the Fonda del Rio—was pretty run down. So was the plaza, for that matter. Struggling trees and a lot of bare dirt.

"You can't order just anything," said Mrs. Curtis inside. "We have a deal here. You get the enchiladas or the chicken."

Mrs. Curtis was nice enough, and she didn't hold grudges, but she had some quirks. For one, she looked like she was winking at you because when she blinked only her right eyelid flapped up and down.

"Order your drinks over here," she said. She stood next to a side table in the musty hotel dining room, which looked like it had recently been furnished by an undertaker, and tapped her right forefinger on a long pad of paper. It was her other quirk: that finger tapped away on her left elbow when her arms were crossed, or on the back of a bus seat, or on the cover flap of her purse.

The rest of the kids had taken their sweet time to get back to the bus, so by comparison Jill and I looked pretty good. "You're prompt, if sacrilegious," said Mrs. Curtis to Jill after the dust-up in the bus.

But the stragglers had made us all late to dinner and Mrs. Curtis wanted us to eat fast. We still had to drive all the way home, clear up the Rio Grande Valley, and it was a five-hour trip.

"How do you do that?" said Linda Ralston, one of Jill's friends. She was a ninth-grader.

"What?" I said.

"Bargain like that." She had watched me buy a striped blanket from a stall along Avenida Porfirio Díaz.

"I just talk to the vendors," I said. "Sometimes they'll come down."

"You haggle," said Linda. "In Spanish. Your Spanish can't be that good."

"Maybe not," I said. "It only works about half the time."

"Who taught you?"

Mrs. Curtis came over to our table. "Chicken, Linda?" she said.

"No," said Linda. "Enchiladas."

Mrs. Curtis went off to her sideboard, where the waitress was making a list. Her hair was done up in a French curl and she was wearing a much-washed white cotton blouse with a purple skirt and a lime-green sweater. She walked with a little limp.

"God, no wonder her husband left her," said Linda. She was smiling. "Colorblind. She's so incredibly out of it." Linda's eyes were dark brown, cool shading into cold, and set pretty close to her nose. She stood around a lot and calculated.

After we ate, a junior preacher who had come along for the ride stood up and spoke about Jesus and the road. Jesus sure had a lot of experience traveling around, he said.

Jill and I got cups of coffee from an urn at the edge of the dining room and sat down to look through our treasures. Their newspaper wrappers were noisy and we held the packages under the table as we unwrapped them and tried to be quiet.

"Who's that for?" said Jill. She was looking at the rolled-up blanket from the street stall that Linda had been fussing about.

"My mother." I unrolled the package carefully. "And this string puppet is for you."

Jill picked the puppet up by his little cross-stick controls. They moved the lines that operated his arms and legs. His left shoulder clacked against the edge of the table.

Mrs. Curtis looked over at us. "Brother Meyers," she said, mouthing the words and pointing to the preacher.

"When did you get it?" said Jill, whispering.

"When I bought the blanket. You were talking to Linda."

"Thanks," she said.

"Do you want to see the rings?" I whispered back, but as I reached for them the bundle of switchblades slipped through my fingers and the knives clattered across the hard tile floor.

"Oh, Jesus," said Jill. She and I scooped most of them up before Mrs. Curtis got to our table. She spied a black stiletto that was lying under my chair and picked it up.

"What's this?" said Mrs. Curtis. She motioned Jill and me out the door. We went over to a far corner of the lobby and she held the knife between her thumb and forefinger. "What is this good for?"

"Don't press the button," I said. "It'll jump out of your hand."

"Are you planning a life of crime, Gil?" she said.

"No, ma'am," I said. "Probably something else."

"Are these legal?"

"Not that I know of, no."

"Well, how did you get this across?—The border, I mean."

"They didn't ask. The Feds. At the State of Texas port of entry they're more worried about you bringing in booze."

"You didn't," said Mrs. Curtis.

"No, ma'am. I don't drink."

"Me, either," said Jill.

"You're still children."

"Please, ma'am," I said, "don't flash that knife around."

"How does it work?"

"May I?" I said.

She gave it to me and I pressed the button. There was a satisfying snap and the silvery blade sprang out into the lamplight.

"Oh, my," said Mrs. Curtis. "You could stick someone with this."

"I wouldn't do that," I said. "You could fish with it if you wanted to. I mean, it would be good for cutting your line off snags in trees."

"Fishing," she said. "That's pretty lame." She turned the switchblade over a couple of times in her hand, and I took it back and showed her how to hold the button down and close the blade.

"Maybe I should keep it for a while," she said. "It's quite dangerous."

"You can have it if you'd like," I said.

"Just for a while," she said, dropping it into her purse. Jill and I looked at each other and went back into the restaurant.

"Jesus will show you the way," said Brother Meyers. "He will calm the roiling waters and quiet all the doubts of the most turbulent mind and the coarsest sinner." He was very earnest. He seemed to be wrapping up.

"We hope to see you in Sunday School sometime soon," said Mrs. Curtis, and she clutched her purse with both hands as she went back to her seat.

"Not tomorrow," I said to Jill. "I have to sell papers."

I didn't drink coffee much at all because I thought it had a bitter taste and a cup of tea was better in the morning. My mother loved tea and brewed it up from loose leaves, usually after work. She sat at the kitchen table and read the paper with a hot cup of orange pekoe and sighed, and I started to like it myself when I got up.

"Just take a shower," she said. "The warm water pouring over your eyes is as good as any coffee or tea." She was right about that, too.

I guess it was the shower that got me going the next morning, and I met Mrs. King, the route manager, at the Catholic church. It was about 7:30. You could still see your breath in the air. The church was a little west of Huttontown Shopping Center, just north of Menaul.

"Here's a hundred twenty-five papers, Gil," she said. "Are you going to stay all morning?"

"Till twelve-thirty," I said. Five masses.

"Good luck." She helped me unload the bundles from the back of her pickup and left.

The amazing thing about the Catholics was that they didn't mind all this. I guess they had never heard that story about Jesus and the moneychangers in the temple. You could stack up the Sunday papers just outside the front door of the church and people bought them in droves as the service ended and they came back out.

The Sunday papers were a quarter apiece and the parishioners almost always gave you a tip. The priest came out once in a while to smoke a cigarette and get some air or stretch his legs between masses and even he would give you a tip.

"Nice morning," he said.

"Yes, it is," I said.

"My name is Burns."

"Gil Wheeler, Father." I shook his hand.

"Anything good?" he said.

"An expansion at the base. Sandia Labs are expanding."

He nodded. "That's more people for Huttontown," he said. "More of a flock for me." He looked off at the mountains to the east. They were a little snowy. People were driving up in their cars for the next mass. "And more papers for you." He gave me fifty cents and strolled back inside, flipping through the sooty sheets till he hit the sports section.

I could never do this sort of thing up the street at my own church. Besides, if I was working I didn't have to show up at all on Sunday morning. I couldn't be in two places at once.

Ned Tilman drove up on his Cushman Eagle with his pal Frankie Morales on the back. They parked under a tree near the door, and Tilman said, "I saw a ring you did."

I was sitting on a bundle of papers reading a book on botany that I had to finish for science.

"Do you make those or do you buy 'em that way?"

"I buy 'em and then fix 'em up."

"How'd you learn?"

"I just sort of figured it out."

"I never heard of anyone polishing rings," said Tilman.

"Do you go to this church, kid?" said Morales. He was quite a jock, the best athlete at Ridgeline Junior High. He had letters in track and football, and the girls thought he was incredibly cool.

"No."

"Then what the hell are you doing here?"

"Selling papers. You want one?"

"Where do you get 'em?" said Tilman. He meant the rings.

I was yawning. The bus had pulled in at about 1:30 the night before. "Mostly over on Central," I said. "A curio place up the street from the Terrace Drive-In. East of Wyoming Boulevard. And sometimes in Mexico."

"Mexico," said Morales. "You don't know diddly shit about Mexico."

Ned pitched me the keys to his Eagle. "Hold on to these for me, will you?" he said. "Till we come out." The organist started up in the sanctuary and they went in.

Ned's Eagle was a '57, and he kept it in perfect shape. The blue tank and fenders had no scratches at all and the chrome pipe was nicely polished. Not a speck of mud. The chain was lightly oiled but not greasy and the tension was just right, not too tight. Ned changed the oil every thousand miles, and he hosed down the engine and the wheels every week. He even rubbed down the seat and the leather pillion with mink oil. "My brother taught me that," he told me once.

Ned knew how to take the baffles out of the muffler and I had watched him do it a couple of times after class. My pal Harold Claus did it to his Eagle, too, and in Huttontown you could hear the two of them going down the streets a half-mile or so away to the sound of a completely satisfying four-stroke roar.

Of course, Tilman put the baffles back in when he came to church.

I put the key in the ignition and kicked up the kickstand and practiced leaning Ned's Eagle from side to side for a few minutes. Left around a corner; right to miss some kid's ball bouncing into the street.

"Do you want to sell me a paper, son?" said a guy with an old-fashioned bill cap on. "Actually, I need two."

"Yes, sir, sure," I said. "Sorry." I hopped off the Eagle and gave him two papers and he gave me a buck and Ned and Morales came out with the rest of the crowd. I handed Ned his keys.

"Catch me after class sometime," he said. "We can drive it around a little."

"Sure, Ned."

"I might want one of those rings," he said. "How much?"

"Three-fifty."

"Sure," he said. "Next week sometime?"

"About Thursday."

"Okay." Ned turned the key and jumped down on the starter pedal and the engine caught with a nice bang. He backed the Eagle away from the tree and Morales got on the back. He was still scowling.

"You know Hiller, kid?" he said.

"Yeah, I know him," I said. That was a kid I had fought with a couple of times at school. A rude little bastard if ever there was one.

"Well, he's a friend of mine," said Morales. "And you're not."

"I don't even know you, Frankie," I said.

"I hope he stomps your ass," said Frankie.

"That what Father Burns was talking about in there?" I said. "Pound thy neighbor?"

"Knock it off, Frankie," said Ned. He gunned his engine. "Thursday, then. See you, Gil."

Business wasn't bad at all that week. Jimmy Fitch picked up the bullwhip right away for his pal and gave me five bucks. I had three rings finished by Tuesday night. A guy named Will Carnes, who I barely knew, took one on Wednesday and Ned picked his up on Thursday. Ray Dailey bought one from me, or started to, for his girlfriend Leah. He was this guy with a beautiful BSA that turned out not to be his after all. His brother Cres had thumped him for wrecking it with me on the back, but Ray seemed to be over that.

You couldn't blame Cres. It was his motor and he was still paying it off.

"That's a beauty, Gil," said Ray. He held the ring up and turned it around in his fingers. "Leah's gonna love it. You're not still mad at me for leaving you up on the mesa, are you?"

"Not really," I said.

"How much?" said Ray.

"Seven bucks," I said.

"Can I give you half now and half next week?"

"Not really," I said.

You could smell Ray's hair from about five feet away. He used La Parot Pomade and it was pretty strong. Most of the rest of us just used some kind of dime store brilliantine or Wild Root Creme Oil on our locks, but Ray had a sharp-looking flattop with swept-back flanders on the sides, always in perfect shape, and it was due to the La Parot, carefully applied.

It came in a little black tin with gold lettering and a red and green macaw on the side.

"Seven bucks?" he said.

"Yeah."

"I'll have it to you in the morning."

I was a little doubtful about that. Even if the deal went through, Ray might be back in a week or two. Leah didn't care for him that much, and certainly if I let him pay in two installments I'd never get the balance due after she kissed him off.

It was an easier deal with my cousin Sonny Wheeler. Sonny and his friends were in high school, very grown up, with Ducatis and Triumphs for wheels, and they all had motorcycle jackets and engineer's boots and Marlon Brando *Wild One* images to polish.

"Did you get those knives, Gil?" he asked me. We were at Dick's Chat and Chew, on Wyoming Boulevard and Claremont at the west end of Huttontown, drinking root beer floats.

"Yeah."

"Where are they?"

"In the knapsack," I said.

"Well, let's see 'em."

"Let me finish this float."

"How much were they?"

"Ten bucks," I said, "but I lost one."

"Here's thirteen," said Sonny.

"What're you gonna do with 'em?" I said.

"Nothin'," said Sonny. "They're just cool. We'll flash 'em around at parties for fun."

"I'll give 'em to you outside," I said.

We walked around to the parking lot at the side of the place, and I pulled the newspaper package of switchblades out of my canvas backpack. Sonny looked at the knives and tried one out. It had a strong spring and it flew out of his hand when he pressed the button. Just like Mrs. Curtis.

"Wow," he said. He gave me an extra three bucks. "For all your trouble."

Sonny was okay. He never really tried to take advantage of you.

I had two bullwhips left and Leo Salisbury took care of those. I think he resold one of them (a ten-footer) to Tommy Newton, because you could hear those guys cracking them in Leo's backyard, which was across the street from my house, for weeks afterward.

"I'm gonna practice till I can snuff out a candle with my eight-footer," he said. Just like Lash LaRue. But Leo didn't really have the patience for that.

As for Tommy, he kept trying to crack the tongue of his whip behind his head. But the rest of it was just too long. Tommy nipped off a fair chunk of his earlobe with one of his long snaps and bled all over a good blue shirt, for which his mother gave him a lot of hell, according to Leo.

I didn't have too much homework that week, and so I was able to work on the rest of the rings pretty steadily every night. I had an old yellow radio that my granddad had given me, and after 7:30 KOMA from Oklahoma City would come in on it very clearly. Well, pretty clearly.

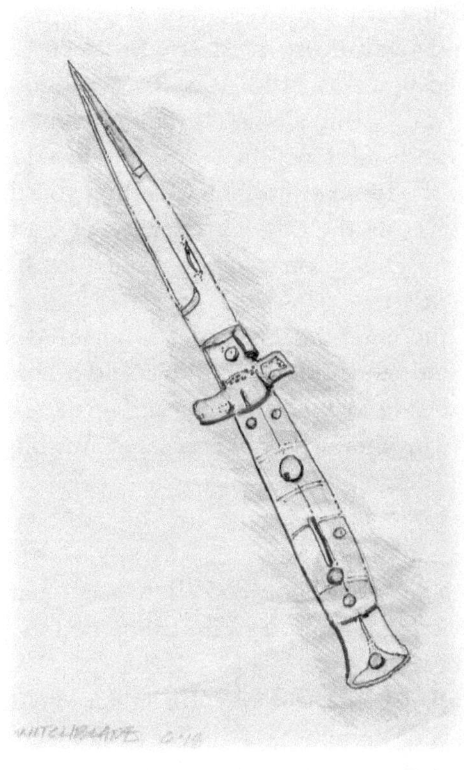

*"They're just cool," said Sonny. "We'll flash 'em around
at parties for fun."*

The songs ebbed and flowed. KOMA played guys like Ben Colder (who was really Sheb Wooley from *Rawhide*) singing stuff like "The Purple People Eater." I liked Dion and the Belmonts, too ("Where or When" was their big smash), and anything by the Everly Brothers.

But the best guy of all was Ricky Nelson, and his best song was "String-along." It reminded me of Marian Calvert, who lived down the street. She loved to get you going, but she thought nothing of letting you down. She wouldn't give me the time of day now, at least not till I had a motorcycle of some sort, but once she had been a champion kisser.

I sat there at the door-on-sawhorses desk in my bedroom and sanded down the rings and hummed to the tunes on the radio as they came and went. And fended off my little brother, who was reading comic books on his bunk.

"Let's listen to something else," he said.

"Let's not," I said.

"When are you gonna stop all that scraping?"

"I'm working, Micron." His real name was Lenny. "I need to finish this stuff."

My dad opened the door. "Turn the radio down. Did you finish your homework, Gil?" he said.

"You never need to ask me. Yeah, I did. Yes, sir."

"What are you working on there?"

"Rings," I said. I showed him one that was almost done. "You have to polish them in a uniform way. One direction. Otherwise, the scratches never smooth out." I was using light emery paper on them.

He held the ring up to the lamp. "What do you do with these?" he said.

"I sell 'em," I said. "At school."

"I thought you were selling newspapers."

"That's at the shopping center. I'll do that tomorrow afternoon."

"What are doing with all the money?" he said, but I wasn't falling for that.

"There's not that much, Pop," I said. "Nothing pays very much."

He nodded and shut the door.

Connie Francis started singing "Among my Souvenirs," and Micron griped again.

"Pipe down," I said. "I'll turn it off as soon as I'm done with this ring."

The windows in the room were open for the night air and Lenny and I could hear my folks talking on the front stoop. Their voices were low, but the sound carried.

"We could re-finance," said my dad.

"Again?" said Mom.

"Or move, I suppose."

"Oh, Stan," she said. "Not so soon. We just got here." It sounded like she stood up. "I'm chilly," she said. "I'm going in to make a cup of tea."

Sonny's mom, my aunt, found the switchblades rattling around inside one of the boots in his closet and boxed him about the ears. He had an extra hidden under his mattress, which he took to a party. But Michelle Donohue, this blonde who had green eyes and ended up being the love of his life, wasn't impressed. "What the hell are you doing with that thing?" she said. "That's not cool." He gave it to his big brother Clint, who took it with him when he went away to the Navy.

Sonny stopped wearing his black leather jacket with zippers, too. "It was just too hot," he told me. But Michelle hadn't liked that, either.

I stopped by Jill's house on the way home from selling papers one afternoon, and her mother opened the door. "Ah, the merchant," she said. "We heard about your bargaining. Did you sell all your stuff?"

"Most of it," I said. I still had a couple of rings left.

"Jill," she said, toward the hallway, "Gil's here."

Jill's brother Billy came in from the patio. "Hey, Ring Man," he said. He was a seventh-grader. "Can I get one of your rings?"

"I guess so," I said. "You have a steady girl already, Billy?"

"Naw. It's just for me."

Jill came in with her string puppet. She made him walk and then he danced to a little tune coming out of the TV and waved his arm. "What do you think, Gil?" she said.

"She loves that thing," said Mrs. Summers. "I didn't know the Mexicans made pieces like that."

"They make everything," I said. "They're an ingenious people."

Mrs. Summers got us all some Kool-Aid. "So, what will you do with all this money?" she said.

"There's not that much of it, ma'am."

"Don't you like to buy things?"

"Well," I said, "I bought these pants." I had on a pair of new corduroys. "I bought my brother a couple of shirts. I got my mom a blanket."

"He's saving, Mom," said Jill. "For a motorcycle."

"Maybe a Cushman Eagle," I said.

"Those are dangerous, Gil, with their little wheels. A lot of the boys around here go too fast. They're unsafe."

"Well," I said, "that's true. But I could get a regular paper route, which is better than street sales. I think I'd do better. And I already have a license. I've had it for a year."

Harold Claus had let me borrow his Eagle to take the sub-five-horse test at Motor Vehicles, and I had passed it the first time.

"More Kool-Aid?" said Mrs. Summers, but it was a little too sweet for my taste and I declined.

Two days later, on a Friday, I went to the bank before I started selling my papers and put in forty-five bucks. I was hoping for more, but I'd had quite a few expenses. I checked the passbook and the new total came to almost $275.00.

On Sunday, I was sitting on a bale of papers beside the church door. It was a bright morning and I had scooted back into the shade of a big ponderosa pine. I was reading again, for my social studies class this time.

Ned Tilman came up, but he wasn't on his Eagle. He was riding on the back of his brother Matt's Tiger Cub—a sweetly humming Triumph if ever there was one. Matt never said much of anything; he had two long vertical slashes running down the sides of his throat, big scars, and his voice was very weak. Ned had talked about it once. "It was an operation," he said.

Matt just went straight in the door. He was a high school guy, very trim looking, with the sort of Ivy League pants that had a buckle on the back.

"That ring worked, Gil," said Ned. "Karen liked it. Thanks." That was Karen French, Steve French's sister, a shy blonde who wore skirts with flounces. She was in my Spanish class. "She's got it on a chain around her neck."

"Nice going, Ned," I said.

"Ned," croaked Matt. He was in the alcove. "Come on."

I sat back down on the papers and watched for customers.

Bobby Hiller drove up on his Cushman Highlander with Morales on the back. Those old scooters had a long, flaring wrap-around skirt over the engine and the rear wheel and no gears. A centrifugal clutch. You just jumped on the starter and twisted the accelerator, which was the right-hand grip, and off you went. Highlanders shook a lot and had no shocks and they would get up to maybe thirty or thirty-five miles an hour.

Hiller's old Highlander was dirty green, with a crack in the skirt that was spot-welded just behind the seat on the right-hand side.

Those two guys were nothing but bad news, at church or not, but I was set for them. I had on a wide belt with a big brass buckle and I pulled it off and wrapped it around my hand with the buckle hanging down.

Hiller knocked down his kickstand and walked over to me. "I wanna ask you something, kid," he said. Morales stood beside him and to his left. "Don't get bugged, okay?"

"What do you want, Bobby?" I said.

"I got another girl," he said. "Her name's Shelly. She goes to Jackson Junior High."

"Good for you, Bobby," I said.

"So, no more Marian," he said. "I got nothin' further to say about her."

Both those guys were standing about four feet away, in front of the bale of papers. "If I were you, I'd back off," I said.

Bobby looked at the buckle. So did Morales.

"You were saying," I said.

"Calm down," said Bobby. "Jesus. Are you the ring guy or not?"

"What do you mean about Marian?"

"I mean I just like Shelly now. That's what."

"Okay," I said.

"I seen a couple of those rings of yours," he said. "Nice shiny brass tops. Something like that would do the trick with Shelly. Besides, I don't want any more of those little trips to see the principal."

I unwrapped the belt from my hand and flicked it back over my shoulder.

"How much?" said Bobby.

"Four-fifty."

"Okay. When?"

"Next Sunday."

"I can give you a couple of bucks down now, if you want."

"It's okay."

"Next week, then," he said. "That's nice shiny brass, the one I seen. But the question is, can the finish last?"

"Yeah," I said. "Sure. It'll last."

"Next week, then," he said. Bobby jumped on the Highlander's starter and put out his toes on both sides of the scooter to steady it.

Frankie got on the back. He looked at me over his shoulder. "You got out of that one okay, kid," he said, and Bobby gunned his engine and they were gone.

IX

Two Politicians

MILES DAVIS was blowing on the trumpet late at night, in the living room. Little swirls of sound, floating over the dry hills of Spain.

They were wonderful tunes, crisp and spare, and I listened to them as I read in my room down the hall. I was barreling through a little book of stories by de Maupassant for my English class.

When I went into the living room the TV was flickering, light blue and gray, and my dad sat in his chair looking at the screen with a cigarette in his hand. He was just in from campaigning.

"You should come around with me, you know. If I win this, we'll be set."

"That'll be nice," I said.

"Where is everyone, Gil?" he said.

"All asleep."

"Mom?"

"Asleep. For about an hour."

He had a neat bourbon in his other hand. The record wasn't loud, but Miles was insistent. The measures were odd and catchy, and in that dark cave of a room he just sounded haunted.

"I just got that," said the old man. "Do you like it?"

"It's not your usual stuff." He liked the Mills Brothers and anything classical. He loved pieces like the "Grand Canyon Suite" by a guy named Grofé.

"Yeah, I like it," I said.

The hand with the cigarette tapped the armrest of the chair along with the music, and little flurries of ash floated down to the carpet.

"Come with me Saturday, Gil," he said. "I'm going to campaign at a car show. Then I have a bricklayers' union forum in the evening. You can hand out flyers."

I liked the music but the smoke was too much. He loved Old Golds. The front room was as foggy as a cold seacoast somewhere, and you couldn't breathe in it.

"I'm working from three-thirty till about six, Dad," I said. "Selling papers. On Saturday, I mean."

"We'll go in the morning to the fairgrounds," he said. "Then I'll pick you up at the shopping center at six o'clock."

"Okay," I said.

"Maybe we can do one of those cross-country hikes," he said. "Up there along the base of the mountains. I don't always have to campaign." He liked to walk out across the open country below the foothills on a bright day, and to tell you the truth it was one of my favorite things to do with him.

"Sure," I said. "Saturday after next."

"Good," he said. He got up to go into the kitchen for another bourbon.

"Night," I said.

I was sitting in the pew in church reading *The Origin of Species* when the preacher cranked up the volume a notch or two.

*Miles Davis was blowing on the trumpet late at night,
in the living room*

"Don't believe for a moment that you can be sure of salvation," he said. "Good works won't bring it to be. Your own profession of faith may be a start. But only the grace of God can make it happen. The grace of God." He was a bit adamant on that point.

"Pay attention," whispered my aunt. "What's that you're reading?"

"Darwin," I said. I had him tucked into the open hymnal so as not to be conspicuous, but that hadn't quite worked. "I have a short paper due in science."

"Can't you do that later?" she whispered.

I closed the hymnal and the *Origin* and looked up. Half an hour to go. An older guy in the pew in front of me was dozing and his glistening bald head was bobbing. His wife tugged on his elbow.

After a decent interval I cracked the hymnal open again.

"Gil," said my aunt, under her breath.

"Right," I said.

My aunt Elizabeth, my dad's sister, mentioned my reading habits to Zoe McAllister, my Sunday School teacher, who in turn mentioned them to me the following Sunday.

"So, Gil," she said. "Did you get your science paper done?"

"It's due Tuesday, ma'am," I said. "I have a little reading left to finish."

"What's it on?" she said.

"How Darwin's observations led him to an explanation of how life changes," I said. "How plants and animals adapt to where they live and each other over time. I'm on my second book by him on natural history. It's pretty good."

"That's a dubious subject," she said.

"It fascinated him," I said.

"Who?"

"Charles Darwin, ma'am. Have you read him?"

"No," she said.

"He makes a good argument," I said.

"So do the *Apocrypha*, but they're equally false. We've known that now for centuries."

"Well, the report's almost done," I said. "It's not too long."

"Let's get on with our lesson here," said Miss McAllister. The other kids were getting restless; they didn't have a horse in this race.

I asked her afterward, in private, if she had read the *Apocrypha*.

"Good heavens, no," she said. "Why would you ask me that?"

"Just a question," I said. "You didn't seem to like it. My folks have a copy of it on the shelf at home."

She tried to look at me sternly for a moment, but it didn't last. She was a pretty brunette in her twenties who worked in a bank, and she had a cheerful disposition. I didn't mind her. My aunt had revved her up with her tales of my inattention in church.

"Let me know how you do with that paper, will you?" she said.

"Sure," I said.

She put her hand on my shoulder. I hadn't grown much yet so she stood over me by four or five inches. "We'll have to keep on churching you up," she said. She smiled at me. Then she went off down the hall to meet Hugh McGee, her sometime boyfriend. They liked to sit in the far back pew, just in front of the wall, and write each other notes during the service. Sometimes they necked a little, and sometimes he put his hand on her leg. He had some kind of job at Korber's Hardware downtown, and he also had a candy-apple-red '48 Lincoln with spinners and chrome dual exhausts. Lake pipes, actually. Maybe you get the idea. He liked to take her to church in it.

When the Sunday morning newspaper job at the Catholic church had come along, I had jumped at it. Bye-bye, Sunday School. It was just a practical thing—I needed the money and I thought I was more or less earning my way. Added to my afternoon paper sales during the week and another thing or two I was working on, it gave me a chance to save a little. I had to have about three twenty-five for a good used Cushman Eagle, and maybe another fifty bucks for insurance and other expenses.

But it wasn't that easy. Unexpected demands for cash always came up.

For instance, some worthless lowlife swiped all the gym clothes out of my locker basket. I think he stuck a crochet hook through the mesh, twirled it into the clothes, and just fished them out. He got all the sweaty stuff, though—I hadn't taken anything home for a week or two to wash it. At least he left the cross-country shoes.

I tried to tell the coach, Mr. Hacker, what had happened, but he was having none of it. He threatened to flunk me if I didn't dress out. You had to go way downtown, ten miles or so from Huttontown, to the right sporting goods store to buy shorts, socks, and a tee shirt, and I could only do that by bus on the weekend. So, I kept my street clothes on for athletics three or four times straight and Hacker hauled me up as an example in front of the whole P.E. class.

"Now here's a guy who ought to have an A in this class," he said. "Maybe a B. But he's gonna flunk if he does this one more time."

That was on a Thursday.

"Maybe I'll have new gear by Monday," I said. "I'll try."

"You'd better, Wheeler," said Coach Hacker. "You'd better."

There must have been thirty guys there, not all of them my friends.

"He's an asshole anyway," said a voice from the back of the group. There was a lot of New York in it.

"Ten laps around the field," said Mr. Hacker. "On the track. All you guys. Go."

I was pretty mad, but I started jogging anyway. About halfway around the second lap I pulled up alongside my pal Jimmy Fitch. "Was it Lefty Mulroney who said that?" I said.

"Yeah," gasped Jimmy.

I dropped back on my pace a little till New York Lefty came up on my right.

"What's wrong with you?" I said. "I never crossed you."

"I'm gonna thump your ass, kid," he said. He took two breaths to get it out.

"I don't think so," I said. "Don't count on it."

Ridgeline Junior High. Brand new school, in a brand-new part of the city. Still smelled like new paint. *More like Frontline Junior High*, I thought.

But the gym clothes were gone, and I had to get new ones right away. That's where the jobs came in handy.

I couldn't ask the old man. He wouldn't have any cash. Besides, he was campaigning.

My mother was a different case entirely. She was a nice-looking woman who never thought of herself as pretty. She just worked doggedly, persistently, fifty hours a week. Sometimes sixty. Maybe she bought a skirt or a blouse once a year for herself. She had big stuff like a mortgage or a car payment or food to think about. And believe me, she thought about it all the time. She grew up during the Depression. You wouldn't want to bug her about chicken feed like gym clothes.

Besides, I had the money already. No need, really, to ask anybody. Some of it I owed to the fact that the Catholics at their new church proved to be very practical and helpful people. Ten-minute sermons, a little singing and chanting, stand up, sit down, pass the plate. In and out in forty-five minutes. The priest was measured as he talked, not much given to ecstatic ranting. The Catholics liked their Sunday papers, bought lots of them, and gave me tips, and I could sit there in the lulls when mass was going on and read a guy like Darwin in peace and nobody cared.

It was a nice break from Sunday School.

I rode the bus down Wyoming Boulevard that next Saturday morning and caught a transfer on Central Avenue that took me west to the university and then on down the hill to downtown. I bought a new gym outfit and then walked along until I found a department store. I got my mom a new scarf. Silk, I think. Bright red.

I was hungry on the way home so I hopped off the bus at the Round Up Drive-In on Central just west of Wyoming and had a hamburger and some root beer.

"Hi, Gil," said Jeannette Bender, my neighbor. "What are you doing over here?" Jeannette was a smiling blonde and the oldest kid in her family. The Benders lived just a little south of my house on McClellan Street in Huttontown. She was nearly nineteen and she had worked at the Round Up ever since I'd known her.

"Back from downtown," I said. I showed her the bag of new stuff.

"Pretty scarf," she said. "For Jill?"

"How'd you know about her?"

"Deke," she said. That was Jeannette's little brother.

"Well, it's actually for my mom."

"Birthday?" she said.

"Something like that," I said.

I finished up the hamburger and caught the Wyoming bus north to Huttontown.

"Well, Wheeler," said Coach Hacker on Monday. "What have we here?"

I had on the new outfit. "I just got what I said I would, Coach."

"Learned your lesson," said Mr. Hacker.

"You might say that," I said.

I got to be student council president in an unusual way. Archie Hampton, this ninth-grader who was the real president, had gone to a party with some of his Sandia High friends at the house of a well-known but rowdy junior. The guy's parents were gone for the weekend to Silver City, in southwestern New Mexico, and they had left cases of beer in the garage. I don't know what they were thinking.

Archie's pals bought enough ice to fill up a galvanized 55-gallon garbage can and they put all the beer in it and lugged it outside. They set up a barbecue grill and a volleyball net and invited over a bunch of girls. Then they started to play loud music and strip volleyball. Every time one side made a point, somebody on the losing team had to take off a piece of clothing.

They must have plied those girls with a lot of beer. It couldn't have been just the hot dogs.

At any rate, the backyard was pretty noisy by 10:30 or 11:00 that Saturday night and one of the neighbors called the cops. I heard from my friend Leo Salisbury that the girls were mostly topless when the police got there, with a few couples actually in the bedrooms, but it was likely an exaggeration. Leo often got carried away. What *was* true was that Archie was very drunk, tossing his cookies into a brass planter on the front porch, and the cops hauled all of them downtown at midnight and called their parents. They telephoned the school principals, too.

Archie was a smart guy, pretty tall for a junior high kid, and the teachers always called him "an achiever." But that was it for him.

"Jesus, Gil," he said. "How do I fix this?"

I thought he was talking about the drunkenness and his arrest, of course. "Well, Archie," I said, "maybe it won't be a permanent problem. Nobody will talk about it next year when you're out of here and in high school."

"I mean Mary," he said. Mary Sanderson. That was his cheerleader girlfriend. "She heard about those chicks with their blouses off in the backyard and now she won't talk to me."

Hampton looked like a young version of Steve Allen, the guy from the *Tonight* show. Horn-rimmed glasses and slicked-back hair.

"Let it settle a bit. Call her in a week."

"Can't. Her old man said he'd shove me up against a wall and knock my teeth out if I even tried."

At a mid-week student council meeting, Mrs. Crook, the council sponsor and one of my teachers, stood up and said, "Mr. Hampton will be otherwise occupied for the rest of the year. Mr. Wheeler, our vice president, is now the new president of this council."

The home-room representatives looked bewildered for a minute or two. Then they clapped politely. A few of them smiled, even the ninth-graders.

"Your gavel, Gil," she said, and she handed it to me.

My rise in politics had been fast, if fortuitous.

Poor Archie just faded back into the somewhat unwashed, churning mobs of kids in the halls, high-spirited to be sure but mostly just wanting to leave after their daylong duel with the books.

My dad didn't much want to fall back into the mob, either.

I went with him to the fairgrounds the following Saturday morning, where he handed out cards that said WHEELER FOR CONSTABLE. They had a Colt Navy Dragoon revolver logo under the letters. "I'd appreciate your vote," he said, as he shook people's hands.

The cars at the show were mostly customized old Fords and some Chevies, nicely done up, but there were also Packards and MGs and even a Henry J spread out under the trees.

"You're not fighting, are you?" said the old man between voters.

"Not much. Some. Only when I have to."

He gave out a card to an older woman who asked us for the time.

"Last resort?"

"Of course."

"Good," he said. "Few things are worth it. It doesn't solve much."

True, but sometimes it kept the hoods from bothering you again.

"How come you're running for constable, Pop?" I asked. "Why don't you run for the Legislature again?"

He had been a state senator and a magistrate, too, but I knew he wasn't interested in that judicial job anymore. He didn't like passing judgment.

"Because the position was open," he said, "and I know I can win it. And it pays well."

A stout couple waddled up on their way to look at the cars, eyeing the two of us closely. "You're not selling something?" said the guy. "'Cause if you are, I'm not buying."

"No, sir," said my dad. He put out his hand. "I'm Stan Wheeler. This is my boy, Gil. I'm running for constable."

The little plump man took his hand and gave it a weak squeeze. "God, a politician," he said to his wife. They took a card and walked on into the show.

"When's the election?" said another guy. He was a beanpole in a blue workshirt and khaki pants with twitchy eyes. He was carrying a couple of days' worth of stubble on his jaw and he had white spittle in the corner of his mouth.

"In about six weeks," said Dad. "November sixth."

"What's your name?"

"Stanton Wheeler. Stan." The old man gave him a card. "Thank you for your vote."

The guy read it pretty slowly and then looked up. "You want to be a cop?" he said.

"Constable, yes," said Dad.

"I'm not registered," said the guy, shuffling off.

The old man gave me some cards and told me to work the other end of the show. It took me about a half-hour to hand them out, which I was happy to do. "Vote Wheeler for constable," I said, as people edged into the shade of the trees. "Vote experience. Vote for Dad." I grinned at them and sometimes they grinned back.

I walked back down the line of the cars to find the old man and it took some looking to spot him. He had gone off maybe half a block from where I had left him and was sitting on a bench under a tree. His legs were crossed at the knee and his eyes were a little dull.

"Pop," I said. "How about lunch? You ready?"

"Sure," he said. He got up, just a little unsteady, and we started off toward the car.

I hated that dullness in his eyes, which were really a terrific sky blue. As we walked along, I glanced at his brown suede jacket. You could just see the outline of the little hip flask in the inside left breast pocket.

He drove up Central to the Mint, a new bar near the Terrace Drive-In, where we ordered corned beef sandwiches. He knocked down a couple of mixed drinks—Manhattans, I think—while we were eating them, and then he started in on a bourbon and water.

"Pop," I said. "We've got to go. I have to get to work."

"Plenty of time," he said. He took another sip. "Don't worry."

He could hardly walk when at last we got outside. It was a terrific fall day, very clear, with a polished blue sky. You could see the trees on top of the long line of the Sandia range to the east. I stood there for a second or two just looking at them. He gave me the keys as we got to the car. "You'd better drive," he said.

"Okay," I said. But to tell you the truth, it scared the daylights out of me. My new license only covered motorcycles under five horsepower.

"Careful," he said, and he dropped off to sleep in the passenger seat.

I pulled out onto Central with a couple of jerks and went down to Wyoming, where I turned north toward Huttontown. No cops, thank God. I remembered to signal. I had driven a car quite a few times out in the boonies, on dirt roads, but not, for obvious reasons, on paved streets in town. And the cops were a big deal: look at what Hampton had just gone through. They would haul me off if bad turned to worse and they would likely take one look at the old man and haul him off, too.

But you couldn't just pull over and stop and hope the tooth fairy showed up. That wouldn't work. You just had to drive.

I got to Huttontown and turned east on Claremont Avenue, where the traffic was as light as you could find. When I pulled up in the driveway and killed the engine, my brother was playing in the backyard. "Open the back door, Lenny," I said. "Do it now."

Lenny kept messing around with some toy trucks on the ground.

"Now, Lenny, goddammit," I said. I opened the passenger-side door and got the old man's arm around the back of my neck. Then I just muscled him up and walked him along and through the kitchen door, which Lenny held open.

"What's wrong with him?" said Lenny, a little loud.

"Shhh," I said. "He's sleeping. Let's not bother the neighbors."

I put him on the couch in the front room and pulled his shoes off. Then I put his keys in a little dish on top of the refrigerator.

"You okay, Lenny?" I said. "Sorry I yelled at you."

"Sure," he said.

"Where's Mom?"

"She went to see Mrs. Bender for a minute."

"Good. The keys are on the icebox. Tell her I'm off to work, will you?"

"Sure, Gil," he said, and he went back to his orange trucks.

The old man never showed up at the shopping center when I wrapped up with the evening papers around six, so he missed his bricklayers' union forum. It was just as well.

I walked down Wyoming to Dick's Chat and Chew and went in for a Coke. The jukebox was playing this French song, "Dominique," by a sweet-voiced woman named the Singing Nun. I think she was a Canadian, actually. I sat down at a table and Archie Hampton came over from a booth where he had been sitting with his brother.

"Gil," he said. "What's up?"

My hands were all black from newsprint and some of it rubbed off as we shook hands. "Sorry," I said. "Newspapers."

"My old man let me come out," he said. "This is the first time." He looked at his inky hand. "How do you get a job like that?"

"Just ask for it," I said. "It's not hard."

"Ask who?"

"Call up the newspaper office. I think they always need kids. You just have to show up," I said. "Day after day."

"Maybe I'll do that," he said.

We both sipped our soda pop.

"They go over the budget with you yet?" he said.

"Tuesday's the day, I think. We've got three or four events to cover."

"You'll have three hundred seventy-five dollars left in the treasury," said Archie. "Mrs. Crook knows." He looked out the window.

I thought I could handle the student council treasury. I had $335.00 in my own savings account, mostly stashed away for a motorcycle, and I was more or less successfully defending it from all comers. I had heard about taxes, though, and was starting to worry about how they might take bites out of the money.

"I think I might transfer to Jackson Junior High. The principal is reviewing my case. My old man is talking about it."

"You ever do anything else?" I asked. "Missed school or anything?"

"Nope. I'm exemplary. It was just the booze at that party."

"How'd it work out with Mary?" I said.

"Not as smooth as I hoped. I showed up at a Spanish Club meeting last Thursday and she was there. The guys all grinned at me. I tried to talk to her in the hall afterward. 'You're just a pervert,' she said. 'And a complete dipshit.'"

"No meeting of the minds yet, I guess."

"Let me tell you something, Gil," he said. "Looking at high school girls with their blouses off may just be worth going through a little trouble. Oh, man." He was chewing on a toothpick. "Sometimes you have to suffer for love, you know," he said.

I got up. "Good to see you, Archie," I said. "Good luck with your dad." I went out the door and up Claremont Avenue toward my house. It was a little chilly and I popped up the collar of my jacket against the back of my neck.

I had to look around for a few weeks, but I finally found a guy named Eddie Altman who wanted to sell his motorcycle. It was a Ducati Bronco, not an Eagle, but a beautiful bike anyway—red tank with gold scallops and a nice chrome pipe. A four-stroke. It sounded great.

"My old man says he's gonna get me a Honda," said Eddie. That was a new kind of motorcycle from Japan. "But I have to sell this one first." Eddie was a ninth-grader with a lot of friends from shop class. A little bit of a smart aleck. We agreed on $285.00, subject to approval by his dad and mine. Not a bad deal at all, because the Bronco was in terrific shape and only two years old.

"No need for you to think about it, Gil," said my dad. "Sure, you can do it." It was ten days before the election.

"Thanks," I said. "Great."

"And we'll find the cash for it. You don't have to maul your savings."

"What about my savings?" I said.

"Well, you've built up quite a little nest egg, haven't you? You told me."

"I don't think so, Dad," I said. "I didn't say anything to you."

"How else were you going to get the cash for the purchase?" he said. "You just told me you had the two eighty-five."

Oh, man. Look where too much enthusiasm could take you. Just drop boulders on my head.

"Of course, I don't quite have it just now," he said. "But I will in a week or so."

My mother was ironing in the dining room while he and I were talking in the front room. She could hear us.

"In fact, if you could lend me forty or fifty for a few days I'd appreciate it." I was staring at him, but I was disgusted with myself for being so stupid and after a second or two I had to glance away.

"It's for campaign expenses."

"Sure, Pop," I said. "Okay."

"Fine," he said. "I'm going down the way to get some cigarettes. By tomorrow, then?"

"Yeah. Okay," I said.

After he left, I went into the dining room to see my mom. She was working over some shirts in her methodical way. The iron clicked as she moved it back and forth.

"Can we cover something like a motorcycle, Mom?" I said.

She finished a sleeve and set her iron up on end. Then she went into the kitchen, where the teakettle was whistling on a burner. I heard dishes clanking, and she brought in a cup of tea on a saucer for herself and another one for me.

"Here you go, Gil," she said.

"Thanks," I said. It was very good hot orange pekoe with a spoonful of sugar, and I blew on it as I sipped it. "Can we cover it?"

She sipped her tea standing and shook her head from side to side.

"That's what I thought," I said. "Don't worry. It's nothing. It'd be kind of good if he won. I'll pull out eighty-five bucks tomorrow and give it to you. You give him what you want."

She just stood there with her fingers over her mouth, the steam blowing out of the iron behind her.

It turned out I was getting worked up over the wrong thing.

A few days later I was dead asleep when the phone rang at four a.m. I heard my mother talking in the hall, and then she came in and put her hand on my shoulder.

"It's your dad," she said. "He didn't come home last night. He's down at the courthouse. He was sleeping in the car beside the road somewhere in the valley and the police took him in. They're sending a car for me. I'll drive him home in our car if they'll let me have it. Get your brother and your sister off to school, please."

"Sure, Mom," I said. I woke up a little.

"I made some tea for you," she said. "It's in a pot on the stove."

"Thanks," I said, but she left and I dropped off to sleep again.

It didn't make the morning paper but it was sure as hell on the second page of the evening paper as I started to sell it that afternoon. CONSTABLE CANDIDATE WHEELER TAKEN IN FOR DWI, said the header. CHARGES PENDING.

I didn't go out on the street medians that day or push sales very hard in the shopping center. It was a slow news day anyway, and I had twenty or thirty papers left over when six o'clock rolled around.

When the election came the next week, Dad lost, and by about twenty points. The cops decided not to charge him with anything after that, and when my mother heard about it she gave my arm a squeeze.

The student council meeting in early November went well. We planned for a dance in the gym—we called those things sock hops, because you had to kick off your shoes—and voted to spend 125 bucks for a band. That left us enough money to buy some special science and history books for the library, with a bit left over for something else before the end of the year.

We were pleased with ourselves.

Mr. Greene, the principal, sat in on the meeting, which only lasted forty minutes. "That was crisp," he said. "Nicely done."

"Thanks," I said.

"You okay, Gil?" he said.

"Mostly," I said. "Yeah, by and large. I think so."

"Good. Keep in mind what we discussed. No more of this fighting," he said quietly. "I expect something better from you."

"Yes, sir," I said.

"I mean it," he said. "Just stay away from those punks."

"I will," I said. "But will they stay away from me?"

"Gil," said Mr. Greene, "figure out another way to handle them. Avoid 'em."

"Yes, sir," I said.

It was good advice, but avoiding those guys after school was like avoiding breathing. *Maybe I'll think of something*, I thought.

"You'll think of something," said Mr. Greene, standing up. He put his hand on my shoulder. "I'm sure of it."

I wasn't.

Stay away from them.

I was walking home along the mesa road when I saw Altman and two other guys standing on the street corner a block or so in front of me. The city, or Huttontown, just ended right there. No more houses. To the east, it was open grassy country clear up to the mountains.

The Ducati Bronco deal had fallen through because too much of the purchase price had slipped between my fingers.

"Hello, Eddie," I said, and I just kept walking.

I suppose I had gone on another twenty feet when this voice behind me said, "Hey, dickhead—is your old man back in jail?"

Jesus Christ. Not again.

I put my books down off to the side of the road. Mulroney, the guy from New York, and Altman stood there smirking. The third kid turned around and walked off down the street.

Temper, I thought. *Temper.*

A motor scooter was coming south down the mesa road behind them.

They didn't move as I walked back toward them.

"Which one of you morons said that?" I was standing in front of Eddie, but sideways. It had sounded like him, showing off for his pals.

"That was some campaign," he said, grinning.

I turned my right shoulder so it faced him. He couldn't figure it out, and when he leaned in a little to look I busted him in the mouth with the back of my fist.

New York Lefty got in a nice swing to my left cheek and knocked my glasses off, but I kicked his knee hard and punched his left ear solidly.

The scooter stopped and Ned Tilman was pulling Lefty back when I looked up. But I grabbed Altman by the lapels and shoved him up against a phone pole. "What did you say, you son of a bitch?"

"Nothin'," he said.

I hit him again two or three times. Pretty hard. "Take it back."

He was crying now.

"Take it back."

Ned pulled me away. "That's enough, Gil," he said. "Let him go."

I looked over at Mulroney, who was holding his ear. "Jesus, kid," he said, "we didn't mean nothin'."

I started after him again but Ned stood in front of me. "Let 'em go, Gil," he said. "I think they got the message."

They turned and went off down the street. "Let 'em go."

Ned bent over and picked up my glasses and handed them to me. My shirt pocket was torn and I had a hole in one knee of my pants.

"You okay?" he said.

"Yeah. Sure," I said, but I just sat down on the ground. He sat down with me. I felt like staying there for a while.

After I caught my breath I thanked Ned for his help. "There were three of 'em to start,' I said. "Eddie's real brave around his friends. I don't know where the other guy went."

"Where's your books?"

"Down there." I pointed down the road.

"C'mon. I'll give you a ride. I hear you like Eagles."

"Thanks."

"You wanna go shoot some pool? At that Dick's Chat and Chew?"

"Maybe about five-thirty," I said. "I need to go and sell my papers."

"Like that?" He pointed to my pocket, which was hanging down. My knee had a cut that was messing up my lower pant leg and I could feel this bump growing on my cheekbone.

"Well, I'll change first, I guess. At home."

"Hop on," said Ned. "Let's go."

"The unexamined life is not worth living, according to some," said Mrs. Crook. Her observations, you had to say, could be pretty good. "It may be a wasted life. This is a theme that we frequently find in our readings for this class. But how often do we pause for reflection in our very busy lives today?"

Not often enough, I thought. She had a point, as always. For instance, it crossed my mind that pounding your constituents would always be poor form.

"And we go so far off the mark when we expect people to be perfect." She paused at the side of her desk and looked at me, or at least at my row of seats.

I raised my hand. "Beg your pardon, ma'am. What did you say?"

"Perfection and its attendant problems, Gil. People can't be everything we expect, can they?"

"No, ma'am," I said. "I suppose not."

I was still thinking about it at lunch, chewing meatloaf and canned white corn in the cafeteria, when

Leo Salisbury said, "There's a sheepherder out there somewhere. Maybe more than one."

"Where?" I said.

"Out at Juan Tabo. North end of the mountains. Didn't you hear anything?"

You could see the Juan Tabo Basin from the north end of the school.

"Wake up, Gil," said Mario Arenas. "Are you comin' or not?"

"Sunday afternoon. We're gonna hike out and find him. He's a Basque," said Leo.

"This Sunday?"

"Yeah. At noon. We're going cross-country. Get your stuff ready," said Mario.

"Basque. A Basque sheepherder? A Spaniard?"

"Yeah. Come on. We've heard about him since we were kids. We're gonna find him," said Leo. "Listen up."

It was good hiking across the mesa on Sunday afternoon. We cut out toward the mountains cross-country, not following the dirt roads, and the late fall day was both cold and sunny. We walked across the rolling grasslands and dipped down into the arroyos. We walked through prairie dog towns, with the prairie dogs and the little burrowing owls sunning themselves as the afternoon warmed up. Almost time to hibernate, at least for the prairie dogs. The owls blinked in the sunlight; their bodies never moved, but their heads swiveled around 180 degrees as they watched us go by.

As we got closer to the foothills, the gray oaks began showing up in the streamcourses, always beside clusters of granite boulders, and we thought we saw a little blue smoke curling up from a hollow a mile or so in front of us.

"This is good," said Mario. "Maybe we found him." He whistled a few notes to himself.

I hitched a sliding canvas pack strap up on my shoulder, and Mario said, "Look." He was pointing at a ridge covered in junipers and piñons, with live oaks down below them. "Under those trees."

A couple of gray shrubs seemed to be moving along the ridgeline to the east. They looked like the rabbitbrush that you found in the arroyos out there.

"Sheep," said Mario.

"Can't tell yet," said Leo.

More of the gray shrubs moved to the top of the ridge and, when we climbed up to look over, two or three hundred of them were spread out up and down the hollow in front of us, all wooly. And there was a little gypsy-style caravan in the bottom with a fire going in front of it and a coffeepot hung by hooks on a tripod over the flames and off to one side a short, scruffy sheepherder in a blue plaid shirt sitting on a boulder.

He was pretty friendly, maybe because he saw we were just kids. He waved us down.

Around the edges of the flock behind him, a small collie worked straggling sheep back into the general mob.

"Buenas tardes," he said.

"Buenas tardes," said Mario. "Dispénsenos, por favor, ¿pero es usted el pastor?" *Excuse us, please, but are you the sheepherder?*

"Si, claro," he said, and laughed. "El pastor de este vado." *Sure I am. The shepherd of this little hollow.* "Ochoa," he said, and we shook hands with him and introduced ourselves.

We talked to him for a while, but we didn't sit down. He had the only flat-topped stone. The sheep bleated and moved in little drifts around the hollow, munching on everything.

He was a Basque, all right. And chatty. He said he had originally moved from San Sebastian, near the Bay of Biscay and the Pyrenees, to somewhere in Nevada. Then he got this job working for a sheepman named Rascón in Bernalillo, just north of Albuquerque.

"Do you like it here?" I said. "¿A usted le gusta aquí?"

"Es un lugar maravilloso, jóvenes," he said. "Con esos peñoles y los acantilados altos de la sierra." He swept his arm up behind him. *What a marvelous place, boys, with those rock outcrops and the high cliffs up there on the mountain.*

His coffee smelled terrific in the chill air, bubbling away at the side of the fire. He offered us some, and we gave him a cheese sandwich. He only had a couple of extra cups, so Mario and I shared. Leo grinned as he drank his down in gulps.

The sun was starting to sink on the other side of the Rio Grande, so after a few more pleasantries we thanked him and climbed up out of the hollow, back over the ridge. Some of the sheep followed along behind us, and as we turned to look back from a quarter-mile farther on there they were by twos and threes in the last of the sunlight, drifting.

The lights started to come on in a few places in the distant city down below, very quiet, blinking.

On the way back we stuck to Juan Tabo Road. It was dirt but pretty well graded, and faster to walk on as the light faded.

"Can you believe we found him?" said Mario.

"One chance in a hundred," said Leo. "I've never seen anything like that gypsy wagon. What was his name again?"

"Ochoa," I said.

The moon came up, butter-yellow, as we were talking. It was over the high line of the mountains to the east.

"Yeah," said Mario. "Good coffee, too." He kicked along a particularly round pebble as he walked. "Amazing," he said. "A guy from Spain all the way out here. And a little house on wheels with a lantern in it. And all those *borregos*. The sheep." He bent over, picked up his pebble, and flung it into the brush. "You just never know what's gonna come along if you look around a little."

"You said it, Mario," said Leo.

I learned later that what Mario didn't know, and none of us could have suspected, was that there had been a Tiwa hamlet in that hollow a long time before, a little hardscrabble Pueblo farming outpost that had lasted maybe a century or two. And every night by the fire, when Mr. Ochoa had added some aguardiente from the caravan to a mug of coffee, he sipped and looked off into the dark and heard the farmers chanting, a long, low hum to his ears, rising and falling among the gray hulking stones.

X

The Horse on the Sidewalk

"I'M ADOPTED," said Deke, standing at the door. "They paid for me through a placement service. They always said my real mom gave me up, but personally I think they knocked somebody over the head in the baby ward and sneaked me out the back door of the hospital."

My sister Jan was standing there at the door looking at him.

"What do you want, Deke?" I said.

"I just thought you'd want to know," he said. "It's all over the neighborhood."

"What do you mean?" said Jan.

"Well, I've been walking around a little," he said. "You know, talking to people."

He didn't see his own sister Cookie coming up the walk behind him.

"What are you doing, Deke?" she said. "You leave those people alone."

"Nothin'," said Deke.

"Like hell," said Cookie. "You're dishing out that stupid 'placement service' stuff again, aren't you? You come with me." She grabbed his scrawny arm.

Deke was the youngest of the Benders. He was only in fifth grade. Cookie was much older, a junior in high school, and by and large they got along. But she was mad this time.

"Hi, Jan," said Cookie. "Hello, Gil. Sorry to bother you. Come on, Deke."

We lived at the top of a little slope on McClellan Street, and as Deke and his sister walked down toward the pavement he pulled his arm away from her. "Don't touch me," he said.

"Go on home," said Cookie. "I'll be there in a minute. Mom wants to talk to you."

Deke lit up as soon as he reached our driveway.

"And don't smoke," she said.

He waved her off and walked away, shuffling his feet.

Cookie came back to the door. "He's not at it again, I hope."

"He just mentioned that he was adopted," I said.

"He did it last week, too," she said.

"Is he?" said Jan. "Adopted?" She was just eleven that April, with light brown hair and eager blue eyes. She always wanted to believe what people told her.

"Of course not," said Cookie. "He and Mom just had a little tiff. So here he is making the rounds again."

Cookie sighed. She was a redhead—brown-haired, really, but with a lot of red mixed in. I guess she was a little stocky, but she was sweet-tempered. She always had a smile for you.

A pink Cushman Eagle pulled up to the curb at the end of our walk. No kidding: *pink*. The tires were baldies, front and back. The Eagle was old and a little beat up, but it wasn't greasy. It made a nice sound. New leather seat.

Cookie turned around and waved. "It's Terry," she said.

"I know," I said. "I know him."

"You do?"

"Yeah. He's friends with a guy I know named Parnell McCann."

"The guy on the Mustang."

"Yeah. That guy."

"Cheryl, you comin'?" said Terry. That was Cookie's real name.

"One second," said Cookie.

Deke had walked past their house and was slinking his way down the block. Cookie pointed at him and yelled at Terry. "Go get him, will you?"

Terry nodded and kicked over his engine.

Cookie had a couple of strands of turquoise heishi beads around her neck. Navajo stuff. She was tanned and the turquoise looked like something out of a magazine against her throat and her yellow blouse.

"Deke doesn't do that sort of thing in class," said Jan. "In fact, he's kind of nice." She looked off down the block in Deke's direction just as he broke into a run with Cookie's boyfriend Terry bearing down on him.

"That's a motorcycle like yours, Gil," she said, and she walked back across the living room to her piano and began to play again. She loved "Claire de Lune" and she practiced it over and over with her foot on the damper pedal. "I don't want to bother people," she said.

"You don't have to press the pedal, " I told her. "Play as loud as you like."

Even at eleven her fingers just danced across the keys, and sometimes I sat there with the window open and the breeze blowing around my neck and listened to her for a while.

"'Claire de Lune' is better muted," she said. She did a couple of bars. "When are you going to give me a ride?"

"Give me a week or two," I said. "I'm still a little wobbly."

It was true. I had just bought Ned Tilman's blue Eagle for $265.99, and I spent a fair amount of time polishing it, adjusting the chain, changing the oil, and fiddling with the tire pressure. I didn't really have to do any of that stuff, because Ned had kept the thing in perfect shape.

"That's a beauty," said Leo Salisbury, when he first saw it.

"Tilman got his brother's Tiger Cub," I said.

"What's the insurance run?"

"Almost fifty bucks. I'm broke now."

It didn't bother me. Now I didn't have to bum rides or walk so far to get my work done. The Eagle had wiped out all my savings, but with a few months' work they'd go back up again.

"Come down and see me, Gil," said the old man. "You'll like this new office."

He was doing better. He had gone to a clinic for a while after a rough patch and come back clear-eyed and coherent. You could actually talk to him and make sense out of a conversation.

He was newly in the real estate business with one of his long-time pals, and they had set up shop in an old title company office on Cornell Street across from the university. The Wheeler-Edwards Realty, they called it. Nice ring to it. They had even sold a house or two.

I drove my new blue Cushman Eagle down to see him late one Saturday morning, and we went to Chisholm's for lunch. It was just two doors away from his office, on Central Avenue.

"Cheeseburgers, please," said the old man when the waitress came up. "Two of 'em. You want a Coke, Gil?"

"Ice tea," I said.

"A couple of those, too," he said.

We sat at the soda fountain counter, which snaked in and out in an elaborate S shape. It probably sat a hundred people.

"It's a nice office, Pop," I said. He had spaces for himself and Mr. Edwards and maybe three or four other people.

"We'll have a secretary by next week," he said. "Then we'll pick up another broker and maybe a couple of salesmen in a month or two."

I liked talking to him when you could see a gleam in his eye and he spoke about the future as an unknown country full of promise.

"Maybe *three* salesmen," he said.

You had to give him pretty high marks for effort.

The college kids around us chewed and talked fast. Some of them had their books open as they took absent-minded bites of their sandwiches. One worried-looking guy—a little older than the others—drank down four or five cups of coffee as he flipped the pages of his notebooks and mined the remnants of a red pack of Pall Malls.

"How about some hot cashews?" said the old man. One of his favorites. We bought a quarter-pound bag of nuts that the cashier scooped out of a rotating tray in a glass display case and ate them as we walked back to his office.

"Bring a book?" he said. "Homework?"

I had brought a little canvas rucksack on the Eagle. "Yeah," I said.

"Well, pull it out. You can read for a while and I'll make some phone calls. Stick around."

"Sure," I said.

Regular stuff. Just a regular talk with your dad. He smiled at me. He had a neat green blotter on his desk with a couple of glass paperweights I'd seen since I was a kid and an ashtray made out of airplane gears from his Army Air Force days. Everything was neatly arranged. There was a new Smith-Corona portable (a manual) off on a side desk that he used for his letters and legal forms. Familiar pictures on the walls, and a diploma or two. Green filing cabinets.

"What's it for?" he said. "The book."

"History," I said.

He nodded and dialed the phone at the same time. "Just sit back and get comfortable," he said. "I'll make a fast call or two."

So routine. I was tempted to poke around in his desk drawers to look for a bottle or shot glasses after he went down the hall to the bathroom. But I thought better of it. *It's just a Saturday noon in the spring,* I thought. A guy and his kid in an office talking about everyday stuff with the sun coming in through the western windows. Amazing.

Enjoy it while you can.

We had no carport or garage at our house on McClellan Street—just a concrete slab that came to an end at the outside edge of the kitchen.

I drove my Eagle to the top of the driveway on Saturday night after work and parked it in front of our car, pretty close to the back door.

I couldn't get going in the morning. The alarm went off and it felt like I was swimming up from the bottom of the sea as I stuck my hand out to shut it up.

A shower cleared the fog a little. I had to be down at the Catholic church to sell my papers around 7:30.

I ate an egg sandwich and knocked down a cup of tea and went out the back door.

No front wheel on the Eagle, which was lying on its side.

I walked out to the street and looked up and down. No noise, of course. Nobody out. One guy half a block away was backing out of his driveway. No one on a motorcycle, or a scooter. It was a quiet Sunday morning everywhere you looked.

My mom gave me a ride down to work, and it was a good day with the papers. I sold just about everything— only one or two crumpled unsellables left. But I couldn't stop thinking about the Eagle. Who would have enough guts to come right up to your house and swipe a wheel? The bastard had scratched my gas tank on the left side, too. A pretty deep gash. Maybe with a belt buckle or a wrench.

The cops were no help when they came that afternoon. "Should have locked it up," said the shortest of the two. "Especially the wheel." The other guy was making notes.

"How do you chain up a solid wheel?" I said.

"We'll keep our eyes peeled, kid," said the short guy. He gave me a blurry yellow carbon copy of their notes. "Nice Eagle," he said, "except for that scratch."

I called the regular Cushman Eagle dealer downtown the next day after school. $34.95 for a new rim and tire. No, you couldn't pay it off over a couple of months. Cash on the barrelhead.

I called the insurance guys. "You don't have theft insurance, Mr. Wheeler," said the woman at the other end of the line. "You have liability insurance. Did you get in a wreck?"

"No, ma'am," I said.

"Well, call us if you do."

I had about twenty-five or thirty bucks in the bank again, but I sure didn't want to pull it all out. I had no cushion. I'd owned the motor for only two or three weeks and it was expensive to run. I couldn't save up as fast as I liked.

By Tuesday it struck me that I had to get a chain and a lock. My old bike had been swiped the year before and I was beginning to catch on that the cop was right. It was a good idea. There was a steel clothes pole in our backyard, maybe ten feet away from the door, and it was anchored in concrete in the ground. It looked like a spinning umbrella. Very sturdy. If I didn't chain up that Eagle pretty quickly the whole thing would be gone next time.

In the cafeteria at school the next day I was eating lunch with my friend Jimmy Fitch. He lived just down the block and around the corner from me.

"You been over to those new stores yet?" he said. "At Menaul and Eubank?"

A little cluster of shops had popped up at that intersection, a strip center, and it was only about five blocks southeast of where Jimmy and I lived. It was at the far upper edge of Huttontown.

"Not yet."

"Well, go," said Jimmy. "There's a new hardware store there next to the Mexican restaurant. That guy'll have chains."

I thought I'd try to walk up there after I finished with my papers in the afternoon. But it was too far, and when I got to Eubank and Menaul the hardware store was closed. The brand-new restaurant next door was open, though. It was called Taco Sal's, and people were streaming into the place. It had yellow walls and warm yellow light, and you could see the grills and the steaming pots of sauces and beans and rice behind a long stainless steel counter that separated the diners' seats from the kitchen proper. A tiny woman in a fiesta skirt and a white blouse was greeting the hungry as they came in. She carried a handful of menus. The door would open and you'd hear her say, "Hi, Doll," or "Hi, Hon."

"Hi, Sal," they said, and she would lead them off to a table with tiles grouted onto its top and a little flickering candle inside a red glass bowl. Big quarry tiles on the floor, too.

You could smell that café three blocks away, and it made your mouth water. It smelled like rellenos and enchiladas. Hot cheese and chopped onions and bubbling red chile.

I had five or six bucks in my pocket and I was awfully tempted to eat something.

But not that night.

"Hi, Deke," I said. He was sitting on the curb in front of his house as I walked home.

"Hi yourself," said Deke. He was drawing something on the sidewalk with colored pieces of chalk. A pony with a long mane.

"Been at it long?" I said.

He just grunted.

I started to walk off when he said, "Sorry about your wheel."

"You heard about that?"

"Uh huh," he said. "I hear about a lot of stuff." He had a pretty impressive sidewalk horse going. The horse's left front hoof was lifted up smartly and his tail was flying.

A '40 Ford with black rims and baby moons drove up and parked in Deke's driveway. It was maroon. Jeannette,

He had a pretty impressive sidewalk horse going

BHM, after Eric Nyquist

Deke's oldest sister, got out of the passenger side, laughing, and went around to the front of the car. The guy she was with got out and walked around to meet her. It was Albert Enfield, the oldest of a bunch of Enfield brothers, and he put his arm around her waist and walked her up to the front door.

The Enfields ran a sheet metal shop in Old Town, something their dad or granddad had started back in the forties.

Albert had sideburns down to his jawline, and he was wearing heavy engineer's boots and a white tee-shirt with the sleeves rolled up. "Deke," he said, and he waved in our direction.

"He's a hood," said Deke, working on the horse's belly, "but Jeannette's gonna marry him anyway."

"You don't like him?"

"I didn't say that. She's been goin' with him for three years. He's not bad."

"Gotta go, Deke," I said.

"The guy who got your wheel drives a pink Eagle," said Deke.

"A pink Eagle. You mean Granger?"

"I didn't say that."

"He's got a lot of nerve," I said. "What in hell did I ever do to him?"

"I don't know about that," said Deke, "but that motor of yours 'll just walk off in a few days if you don't watch it." He worked over the pony's tail.

I didn't want to say anything more. Deke was an awfully little kid to be so completely plugged in.

"I've always thought there ought to be a reckoning," I said. "Maybe a time when a few things or maybe everything in your life would come to a head. Some kind of resolution."

We were eating dinner, but I had lost my appetite and I put my fork down and looked at the old man. He was looking pretty spiffy in his white shirt and neat bowtie.

"You want me to help you solve that problem with your motorcycle?" he said.

"No. I don't."

He ate some more of my mom's good beans. "Well, what *do* you want?"

"I think I know who came up to the back door and swiped my wheel. It's a high school guy who goes with Cookie Bender."

"Who's Cookie Bender?"

"She lives down the street."

"How do you know this?"

"I just know. From talking to people. Look, I'm used to dealing with junior high kids. But this is a high school guy. He's got a '56 Eagle, and he's a lot older than me."

"Have you seen your wheel on his motorcycle?"

"No."

"Can you get a good look? Pass the cornbread."

"Maybe."

"Then you don't know for sure. Be careful," he said.

"I always am."

"And about reckonings," he said. He sipped his coffee. "Don't hold out for anything like that. They're pretty rare, you know, and when they do happen the process is not what you think it will be."

"What do you mean, Pop?"

"Resolutions in life come at you out of left field," he said. "You won't see 'em till they're on you. And they're never very tidy." He got up to pour himself some more black coffee.

A little of my appetite came back and I finished my plate. Even the cornbread.

◊ ◊ ◊

On Friday my papers sold very fast and I was done by 4:30. I walked as hard as I could up Menaul to the new little strip center, which was about a mile east, and went into Donahue's Hardware. I got a six-foot length of thick chain and a padlock and paid for them at the counter. But behind the counter, up against the wall, Mr. Donahue had two new Eagles. One was green and the other was yellow. And he had lots of parts. A nice supply.

"How much for a front tire and rim?" I asked.

"Twenty-four ninety-five," he said. "Fits everything from fifty-six to fifty-nine."

"Can I give you ten down?" I said.

"Sure," he said. "I'll hold it for you. You got two months to pay it off. Lemme get your name and address."

Progress.

When I got out front, Terry and Cookie were just pulling up to Taco Sal's on his Eagle. He killed the engine and flipped down the kickstand and parked smack in the middle of an empty bay.

"Hi, Gil," said Cookie.

"Hi, Cookie."

Granger's front tire was brand-new—or at least it still had a lot of tread left on it—and the wheel rim was flat blue, not pink. "Somethin' on your mind, kid?" he said.

"I guess not. Somethin' on yours?"

"Don't be lookin' at my Eagle," he said.

I had about eighteen inches of chain hanging down from my right hand and I thought pretty hard about whacking him a few times with it.

I didn't, though.

He wore this long, more or less greasy pompadour and it made his blond hair look like a helmet. His eyebrows were arched as part of his smirk and there was a cigarette hanging out of the side of his mouth. He was a full foot taller than me.

"What's the chain for?"

"Come on, Terry," said Cookie. She pulled on his elbow.

"I ast you a question, kid," he said.

"It's kind of an equalizer," I said, "against guys like you."

He took a swing at me and I just ducked. But his arms must have been a foot longer than mine, because he put his boot behind my right ankle and just reached out and shoved me over backwards. I never laid a hand on him.

"You asshole," said Cookie. But she was yelling at him, not at me.

Granger turned around. "Come in if you want," he said. He walked in the front door of Taco Sal's and looked back at Cookie. "Or don't. I'm hungry."

Cookie waited a couple of minutes to see if I was okay. I was. That shove only took the wind out of me. It confirmed all my past experience with scuffles: if you don't pound the other guy fast and first you don't have a chance. And if the other guy outweighs you by thirty pounds, you will, without question, have the hell knocked out of you.

"I'm fine," I said. I got up on my feet and slapped the dust off my pants, and Cookie turned and went through the door without another word.

But maybe Cookie stayed mad. I didn't see Granger driving down the street to the Benders' house for about ten days.

Deke came over and talked to my sister Jan a lot. It was mostly when she was playing the piano, and once he took her up to the IGA grocery store a block away and bought her a Coke.

When she came back, after a half-hour or so, she said, "They're all kind of bent out of shape over there." She was talking about the Benders. "Cookie doesn't like that guy on the motorcycle any more. She told him to get lost."

I didn't blame Cookie. I didn't exactly like Granger myself, but I couldn't quite figure out how to nail him for stealing my wheel without losing my teeth. It's not easy to prove that a wheel is yours.

"Something else, though," said Jan.

The '40 Ford rumbled up to the Benders' drive down the block and Enfield got out with another guy. It looked like his brother Kyle, who was a little younger than Albert. They went up to the front door and knocked. Albert shifted his weight from foot to foot, spat, tugged on his pants, and looked in the windows. The little brother lit up a cigarette and was glaring at Albert or maybe just at the locked door. His shoulders were hunched up and he looked like he could eat a dog. I couldn't imagine getting closer than fifty yards to guys like that. Only a very dim bulb would trifle with them.

"Deke says that high school guy Granger has been working for them," said Jan.

"For the Enfields?"

"Yeah. In their sheet metal place. Albert and Jeannette have been fussing about him lately."

"Don't you mean Cookie?" I said.

"No, Jeannette," said Jan. "Cookie broke up with him two weeks ago."

I did okay with the papers over the next couple of weeks. I paid off my new wheel and tire and even put an extra ten bucks in the bank. Things were looking up.

My friend Salisbury, the budding urban theorist and motorcycle restorer, took a seven-transistor radio to school to use in his science class as he talked about transistors versus tubes, but it ended poorly. "Some jerk lifted it when I left the classroom for lunch," he said. "The door was supposed to be locked, too."

"Sorry to hear about it," I said.

"Like your wheel," said Leo. "I worked a couple of months to pay for that." He was fiddling around with an old shortwave in his garage, testing stations on the 25mm band, but all he got was static and buzzes. It was still late afternoon. Too early. "It has to do with these suburbs, you know. I've been reading about it. It may be that loose social organization is natural in a new community that's just sprung up. Nothing's settled. The ties that bind people together aren't knotted yet."

"Maybe," I said. "Sure. That makes sense, I suppose. Or it could be that we just have a select group of low-life maggots in this part of town."

"Uh huh," said Leo, and Radio RSA from South Africa came through the buzz clear as water. "Could be that, too."

I unwrapped a couple of bundles of papers the next afternoon and went over the front page. SANDIA HIGH JUNIOR FALLS OUT OF PICKUP DURING JOYRIDE, it said, lower right, near the bottom. MULTIPLE INJURIES.

The guy was hauled off to the hospital in an ambulance.

"We weren't goin' that fast," said the driver. "But that road has a lot of dips and rises. It's like a roller coaster. I thought he was hangin' on back there in the bed, but I guess not."

The guy speaking was Albert Enfield. *"My brother Kyle was back there and he didn't get tossed out. He's just fine."*

"That's right," said Kyle. "No injuries."

They had been driving north on Juan Tabo Road, all dirt and very bumpy, at the base of the mountains. Must have been at a pretty good clip.

Granger was the guy in the ambulance.

"What's a spleen?" said Deke.

I had my Eagle down at the end of our driveway, on a flat spot next to the concrete. I was sitting on an upside-down milk crate. I had a little bottle of touch-up paint from K-W Auto Supply and I was using the flat end of a book match to mix it into the scratch on my tank. It was working pretty well.

"It's a vital organ," I said.

"That touch-up looks good." Deke put his finger out to feel it.

"Not yet," I said.

"Terry's spleen's smashed," said Deke. "Half his teeth are gone, on the left side. He's all scraped up. His little finger got bent back to his wrist."

I finished the last of the scratch.

"His leg's busted, too," said Deke.

I looked up at him. "Don't stand too close if you're gonna light up," I said.

Deke put the cigarettes back in his shirt pocket. "They threw him outta that truck," he said. "Kyle and Albert. They were doin' thirty-five or forty down that road."

"Why?" I said.

"He was stealin' sheet metal from 'em. And fittings. Sold those things to some other shops."

I glanced over Deke's shoulder as he was talking, and Albert came out of the Benders' house and walked over to the back end of his Ford, which was parked on the street. He popped open the trunk, took out a little box about eighteen by eighteen, and banged it shut again. Then he started up the street toward us. Actually, straight toward me.

This is my motor on my property, I thought. *He's just coming to see Deke.*

Deke spun around. "Hi, Albert," he said.

Enfield walked right up to me. "This yours?" he said. He opened his cardboard box.

My wheel and tire were inside.

"Looks like it," I said.

"I thought so," said Albert. He gave me the box.

"Thanks."

He just walked off.

Deke was running his fingers over the gas tank again. "Terry's not gonna get out of the hospital till nineteen eighty-five," he said. "And Cookie hates him. Now what in the hell am I gonna do for cigarettes?"

XI

Jobs I Have Known

McCann had enough to pay me, but he was stalling for time.

I threw the morning route and he threw the afternoon route in the same neighborhoods, and he had asked me to take over for him while he was gone for a couple of weeks over Easter. How he got that time off from school and where he went with it he never said. Out of town somewhere, I guess.

So I threw his route for him. No misses, no complaints. I even handled three or four starts for the guy, stopping as I went down the street and putting the paper right up on the porch in every case. The new subscribers liked that.

"Thanks, Wheeler," he said, the Monday he got back. "I'll pay you tomorrow."

"Sure, Parnell," I said. "Twenty-five bucks."

"Right," he said.

"I'll be expecting it."

Two weeks later the guy was still dodging me.

He had the most Confederate name I had ever heard—Parnell Johnston McCann. He should have been frying chicken for Stonewall Jackson with a name like that. I asked him about it once, and he said, "Yeah, you're right. I'm from Mississippi. Well, my dad is."

Parnell was one of those guys who treated school as a general suggestion, and a pretty poor one at that. He detested English and math in particular. "I got a job lined up in a tire shop," he said. "But they won't take me till I'm seventeen."

That wouldn't be very long, because he was already sixteen. He had spent a couple of extra years in junior high because of his finely cultivated indifference. Parnell was only about five-six, but he had a pair of snap-top black shoes that he wore with his white socks and jeans. Elvis Presley shoes. The heels were pretty tall (we called them "elevators") and he had taps on them, so he was noisy when he walked. The tall heels gave him a little edge.

Parnell threw his route on a snazzy new Mustang, a cool-looking rumbling three-quarter-scale motorcycle with solid wheels.

I was fairly new to my own paper route—I'd only had it for a few months—and I liked everything about it except getting up so early every day to throw it. At 4:30. You had to put on a sweatshirt and a heavy jacket and gloves, but even then your fingertips and your ears froze.

The job came to me out of the blue.

My cousin, Sonny Wheeler, called me up one day and said, "Gil, I'm quitting the papers. I gotta study more." He was in high school, and I think they were loading him up with homework. "You want the route?"

"Sure," I said. It happened just like that.

When I mentioned it to my mother, she said, "You can't do both, Gil. You can't work in the afternoon, too."

That was all right with me. Eating the car exhaust every day while you were hawking papers in the medians at Huttontown Shopping Center had just about lost its glamour. A day or so earlier, some guy had veered out of his lane, out of control, gone across the median right behind me, and hit a building on the other side of the road.

Probably drunk, although it was only four o'clock.

So I quit selling the afternoon paper.

"You'll make more money, too," said Sonny.

I could kind of build my reserves back up, and pretty fast, too. So, my morning route was fine, but Parnell was still avoiding me.

Sort of a quiet evening.

The phone rang down the hall.

"Gil, it's for you," my sister said.

I left my schoolwork (it was algebra, which I wasn't sorry to leave) and went down the hall to the kitchen and picked up the receiver.

"Whatcha doin'?" said the voice on the other end. It was Jill Summers.

"A little math."

"What else?"

"Looking at a science book—*The Chemical History of a Candle*, by Michael Faraday."

"Any good?"

"Real good."

"I'm reading Henry James," she said. "*The Turn of the Screw*. I'll have to write a little report."

"I haven't read him," I said, "but that's a ghost story, isn't it?"

"Yup. It's creepy. Wanna go to church with me on Sunday?" she said.

"No. Thank you."

"Listening to anything?"

"Yeah." I had a little 45 turntable back in my room. "Ricky Nelson. 'String-along.' And 'Peter Gunn.'"

"Oh. Duane Eddy."

It was a very catchy guitar piece.

"Yeah. And a couple of others. The Everly Brothers."

"Just a minute." She put the phone down and talked to someone in the background. It sounded like her brother, Billy, bugging her about something.

"Billy says hi," she said. "He says, 'How's your Eagle?'"

"Running fine," I said.

"How about Saturday, then? Take me somewhere."

"Okay. What about your mom?"

"It's all right. She thinks you're a good driver. Maybe in the morning? Ten o'clock?"

"Okay. Sure," I said.

"Oh. My neck is itching." You could hear her rubbing it over the line. "A bug got me just above the collar."

Jill had soft long fingers, the first thing I ever noticed about her, and I could see her in my mind's eye flicking them back and forth on her neck and across one of the cashmere sweaters that she looked so good in.

"Show me those sheep," she said, "on Saturday."

"In the foothills?"

"No. Not the tame ones. The bighorns you told me about. Up on the Sandias. On top."

"It's twenty or thirty miles," I said.

"Show them to me," she said. The radio was playing softly somewhere behind her. It was KOMA, Oklahoma City, which you could pick up at night.

"I'm gonna get back to Henry, Gil," she said. "I have to finish. I was just thinking about you. That's all."

"I've been thinking about you, too."
"Saturday, then."
"Saturday it is."

Johnny Fenwick, a friend of mine who owned a Ducati, was rolling papers with me on Saturday morning. Our routes were next to each other, and we met the route manager at a Humble station at Constitution and Wyoming. The owner of the place was a friendly guy, and he let us sit outside on a planter wall as long as we cleaned up the mess we always made getting the papers ready for delivery.

"I'll see you at that bakery at Huttontown when you get done," said Johnny. "They got doughnuts."

We usually finished about 6:15 or 6:30. "Are they open that early?" I said.

"Out back," said Johnny. "Damn."

"What's wrong."

"Cut a crease in my little finger," he said. He was snapping his right hand. The three-ply string we used was like that. You ran it three or four times around the rolled-up paper, very fast but not very tight, and popped it with the back side of your hand. Then you pumped it down with the palm of your hand toward the middle of the rolled-up paper.

But even two-ply string would slice you. Masking tape worked sometimes, wrapped around the second joint of your little finger. If you remembered to put it on in the morning blur.

"How many are you throwing now?" I said. "Papers."

Johnny was almost done.

"One sixty-one," he said.

◊ ◊ ◊

I finished up about forty-five minutes later and drove down Wyoming to the center. It was dead out front, but around back it was pretty lively. Trucks were pulling up to the rear doors of the shops and unloading their deliveries, and clerks and stockers and owners parked and unlocked doors to get their businesses ready for the day. Eight or nine pallets were lined up behind the bakery, loaded with sacks of flour and sugar, cans of shortening, and boxes of Fleischmann's Yeast, and the back door was open. The smell of fresh bread mixed with the greasy sweet aroma of hot bubbling doughnuts poured out into the parking lot.

Johnny was cramming doughnuts into his mouth and watching a police car with its bubble gum machine flashing. It was parked a little to the west. The cops were talking to Mr. Cox, the pharmacist, behind his drugstore. He was pointing to his front bumper with one hand and waving the other in the air.

"He hit this guy next door," said Johnny. "Hit his car, I mean. He kind of sideswiped him and then just drove on."

Mr. Simpson, the guy who owned the shoe repair shop, was rubbing the paint on the side of his Chevy. It was a blue '57 two-door hardtop. He looked up and nodded at me.

"Cox thought nobody was looking," said Johnny. "But I was."

"You saw it?"

"Sure," he said. "About twenty minutes ago. The cops asked me, and I told 'em. They told the shoe repair guy. He was inside his shop."

A motorcycle rumbled up behind the pallets with its lights on.

"Morning, Parnell," said Johnny. "How's Steph?"

That was Stephanie, Parnell's sister, Johnny's girlfriend.

"Oh, Jesus," said Parnell. I was standing next to Johnny as we watched the cops.

"Parnell," I said.

"I don't have your money, Wheeler," he said. "I just came down here to get some stuff for breakfast. For my mom."

"That's okay, Parnell," I said. "I'll be out collecting for my route this afternoon and I'll just swing by and ask your old man for it. Or maybe your mom."

He pushed by Johnny and me and went into the bakery. A policeman came over to Mr. Simpson's car to look at the damage, and as the sun began to rise over the mountains you could see Cox's scrape marks all along the driver's side of the Chevy.

"What does he owe you for?" said Johnny.

"Throwing his route a few weeks back. He's welching."

"He's a welcher," said Johnny. "By the way, Steph loves that ring you sold me."

They had been going steady for a couple of months.

"Show me how you make 'em sometime."

"Sure," I said. But the ring business seemed to be fading away, to tell you the truth. Everybody who wanted to go steady at Ridgeline Junior High was going steady.

"I think I could sell 'em over at Jackson Junior High," he said. "I got some contacts there. It might be fun to be in that business."

Fenwick was a sharp and likeable guy, so that just might work. If he were salesman enough.

"I'll tell you, though, Johnny," I said, "I kind of have my eye on the grocery business. I wouldn't mind being a sacker or a stocker. Maybe learn how to set up a produce case."

"Hadn't thought of that," said Johnny. "Throwing papers isn't bad, though."

"Not at all," I said.

Down the way, Mr. Cox had stopped waving his arms. He was standing still, with his hands in his pockets, while the cop wrote out something on his clipboard.

"Mr. Fenwick," said the other cop in our direction. "Hey, kid. You called this in." He was standing beside Mr. Simpson's car.

Johnny walked over to see him.

Something brushed against my back. It was McCann, carrying a big sack full of doughnuts and bread.

"Don't make me look bad, Wheeler," he said, "in front of anybody."

"Lookin' bad's not the point, Parnell," I said. But meatballs like Parnell never got that, or cared.

"What the hell are you talkin' about?" he said.

"The point is we had a deal. That's the question. Pay your bill."

He kicked over the Mustang, put the sack of bakery goods on the tank, and drove off.

Mr. Simpson tucked the corner of his apron into the front of his pants and leaned against his car door. He shook his head. "Paid it off, too," he said to Johnny and the cop. "Two months ago."

The top of the mountain was misty, with clouds moving through the trees. Eleven thousand feet.

"You have to be quiet, Jill," I said. "They'll spook."

It was chilly up there. Early spring. She buttoned the collar of her jacket and followed me through the firs. "How far?"

"It's maybe a mile."

Big patches of old dirty snow were oozing around the edges of the trees, and young yarrows and clumps of green grass were starting to peek out.

We had parked the Eagle behind a thicket of chokecherries down below Sandia Crest. I was taking her to a place called Kiwanis Meadow. It was just beneath a stone cabin that sat right on the edge of the mountain. Look off to the west when the sky was clear and you could see the Rio Grande valley running sixty or seventy miles to the south. The bighorns liked the meadow in the morning, and if there weren't too many hikers you would find them browsing and calling to each other like sheep do anywhere.

"Colder than I thought," she said, but quietly.

"Not too far now," I said.

The sheep weren't quiet: a ram and four or five ewes, and three lambs. They browsed at the edge of the meadow, half in the trees, and the ewes called to the lambs.

"Oh, my," said Jill. "Look at them." We crouched behind a boulder, and she grabbed my arm. Squeezed it, really.

"You brought me here," she said, under her breath, but they heard her anyway. They stopped chewing and put their noses up, sniffing the air.

But we were still, and the bighorns stayed for another ten minutes.

A couple of loud guys with backpacks and heavy boots came out of the woods on the far side of the meadow, laughing, and that was what sent the bighorns away at last, downhill and into the trees, gone in the wink of an eye.

I didn't want to face the impatient trucks again on North Highway 10, on the east side of the mountains, so I took Jill back toward town along the north side of the Sandia range, through Las Huertas Canyon.

It warmed up as we got lower, and I pulled over in the sunshine to the edge of Ellis Creek, which was cascading next to some limestone cliffs.

"Anything to eat?" I said.

"I'm starved," she said.

She had packed my rucksack with deviled ham sandwiches, my favorites, and a couple of bottles of Royal Crown Cola.

The cliffroses were blooming in the rocks, and the sand plums along the creek, and little butterflies the color of sulfur flitted from stone to stone just above the current.

"Never been here," she said, taking it in. "Never knew this place was here." She looked around and smiled. You could smell the stream in the canyon bottom, a damp smell, of course, a little like mint, and Jill smelled good, too, a little rosy.

She kissed me on the cheek, saying "Thanks" under her breath, and I kissed her back a couple of times, on the mouth, nice ones. Very nice. I've had very few since that were as good. We both dropped our sandwiches.

"Are you still selling those rings?" she said.

"A few. Not too many lately."

"Any left?"

I pulled back from her to see her eyes and she looked up and we both turned a little red.

"I might be able to find one," I said.

"You don't still like that Marian, do you? Or is it Marilyn?"

"Marian. She's going with a guy named Robert Lipton now," I said. "Going steady with him. This week, anyway. I liked her once."

"Well, my mom's gonna be worried," she said. She stood up and brushed off her jeans. She had on one of her soft sweaters, a fuzzy green one that felt as good as it looked, and she brushed that off, too, and pushed her hair back. "He's one of those twins with red motorcycles," she said. "Robert Lipton."

"Are you still selling those rings?" Jill asked

"Jawas, yeah. His brother's name is Raymond. They're in high school now."

"I know them," she said.

"Come on. I'll get you back."

She was rubbing my forearm. "Ring business," she said. "What made you think of it?"

"Just thought it up," I said. "I needed the money."

"You're not very shy with most things, Gil," she said. "You've been pretty good at school selling romance." She leaned over and kissed me on the cheek again. Then she touched my cheek with her hand. With her fingertips.

Jesus. No one had ever done that to me.

"Hop on," I said.

By four o'clock, I was out collecting for my route. I had on my carpenter's apron with the route book stuffed in the side of the deep pouch and a bunch of ones and fives and change jammed in the other end. It was maybe the best time to catch people, and they were mostly in a good mood because it was the weekend. Some of them even paid me for weeks of papers in advance.

People were mowing lawns and rinsing cars in their driveways, and in one yard a bunch of kids had a terrier in a galvanized tub full of warm suds. He kept bouncing up and they kept stuffing him back in and he finally jumped out and ran around the corner of the house, shaking water everywhere.

I parked my Cushman at the end of a block and walked up one side, door-to-door, and then back down the other. The route was in Snow Heights, just down the way from Huttontown, and it was all regular houses except for a couple of three-story apartment buildings.

Most of my customers were just the usual mix of Anglos and Spanish-speaking people, but one house had a German couple who talked in monosyllables and another, at the edge of the route near Eubank, was owned by a red-haired South African Englishwoman named Valerie and her husband, an American who worked down Wyoming Boulevard at the Air Force base. The way she talked was fantastic.

"Cape Town," she told me once. "We're from the other side of Table Mountain. Vineyard district. I miss the sea here, actually." Stuff like that. She sounded like a sort of backwoods Deborah Kerr.

And there was a Chinese guy and his wife, pretty young, on the second story of one of the apartment complexes, down at the end of General Somervell Street. He smiled and paid promptly when I showed up, and it was for a month of papers before I delivered them. Then he bowed and handed over a fifty-cent tip when I gave him change.

"I appreciate it," I said.

"No, thank you," he said, bowing again.

I did a quick count of the collections as I walked along and thought I'd be able to hit a hundred thirty-five bucks in savings by the end of the month, especially if Parnell paid up. Iffy, of course. But that would be good, because the Cushman Eagle had been a lot more expensive to operate than I had counted on. The girls liked it, so that had worked out. Look at Jill, for instance, though I have to say that she had liked me even when I was just hoofing it everywhere. Even Marian Calvert, the great kisser who lived down the street from my house, had been smiling at me again lately and stopping to talk after class.

But you had to pay for all the gas and upkeep and insurance for that Eagle, and none of it was cheap.

There was a car in the driveway at Valerie's house as I started up the walk, so I knew she was home. I heard a motorcycle—a four-stroke—rumbling down the road behind me and turned around.

It was Parnell, coming up the street at half-speed, throwing his papers.

"Parnell," I yelled, but he went by with his middle finger held high.

"Parnell," I yelled again. "Your bags are on fire."

It was true. He had let the right side of his paperbags slip over the blazing hot exhaust pipe of the Mustang and he was leaving quite a trail of smoke.

He stuck his right hand back to grab another paper and pulled out a little rolled-up torch.

He flipped the newspaper through the air. You could hear him shouting something and the Mustang began to wobble. Then he cut the wheel too sharply, hit the curb, and went straight into a fire hydrant.

The guy who owned the corner house on the block was mowing down the edge of his driveway. He killed the mower, grabbed the garden hose up next to his front porch, and sprayed the newspapers and the motorcycle and Parnell until the smoke quit billowing up.

Parnell didn't mind that, of course, because he was out cold, lying in the grass.

"Sweet Jesus," said Valerie, coming out her front door. "What's happened here?" She went back in to call the fire department. She had Frank Sinatra on the stereo, singing through the screen door. *Night and day,* he sang. Somebody was going to be the one.

"Why now?" she said. "It's in the middle of school."

I didn't feel like telling Jill this had happened a few times before. "My dad made a trade," I said, over the phone. "He just traded this house for another one somewhere. I'm sorry."

Actually, I knew that it was even simpler. My dad—or rather my tight-lipped mom with the new crease in her brow—hadn't been able to keep up with the payments. Simple as that.

Jill was quiet for a few seconds at the other end of the line. Then she said, "But you just got that new job. A couple of weeks ago."

And I liked it, too, brief as it was. Of all the jobs I have known, it was up there at the top.

I had stopped in at the IGA grocery store to get some oranges after class one day and Mrs. Griffin, the owner, said, "Gil, did you still want that stocker's job? We have something open."

"Sure," I said.

"Two hours a day during the week, in the afternoon—maybe three—and ten or twelve on Saturday. One twenty-five an hour. It's steady."

I took it in a flash. No more early mornings every day of the week. No frozen knuckles. And they just wrote you a check on Friday. No more chasing people for money all the time.

"I'll have to give my notice," I said, "to the paper company."

"Next week, then," she said. "How about Thursday?"

"Yes, ma'am," I said.

On the telephone, Jill said, "So, when do you have to move?"

"A couple of weeks."

"That's not very long," she said. "Just when things were going so well, too."

We weren't going steady yet, but I could tell from the way I was thinking about her all the time that I might want to ask her pretty soon.

"What'll we do?"

"I'll drive up to see you on weekends."

"From where?"

"I don't know yet. The valley, I think."

She was pretty quiet at the other end of the line.

"Don't worry," I said. "We'll go swimming. At the 'A' Pool. You always like that."

"Yes, I do," she said.

"Maybe some warm Saturday afternoon. A warm day. You can go back and forth across the deep end with that nice backstroke of yours. You'll like that."

"I would," she said.

"I'll like watching you. And I'll get you something to eat on our towels on the grass," I said, "and we can play the radio as much as we want."

"What I want is to see those butterflies again," she said. "Those little whirling yellow wings up on that blue creek in the mountains. With the sound of the water going by beneath them."

I didn't have the heart to tell her that the stream was only at its best in the early spring, just when we had been lucky enough to see it. For the rest of the season it ran on for maybe two or three miles before it was swallowed by the thirsty canyon—water, butterflies, and sound, all gone.

I AM VERY MUCH in the debt of Mr. Zach Hively, the editor and publisher of Casa Urraca Press, for his gracious support and his delight in these stories. Thank you, Zach.

I would also like to thank my friend V. B. Price for his wisdom, friendship, and love of the short story. And for putting me in touch with Mr. Hively. V. B. is a leading connoisseur of Albuquerque and places like Taco Sal's.

My wife, Jo Ann Strathman, and my daughter, Susan Morrow, have kept me supplied with coffee and kind words for quite some time as these stories took shape. Much love.

BHM, 2024

BAKER H. MORROW, a third-generation New Mexican, was born in Albuquerque, where he has lived in both the valley and the heights. After a stint in the Peace Corps, he worked as a landscape architect in his own office and as a professor at the University of New Mexico for many years. He is the author of two other collections of short stories and of *Best Plants for New Mexico Gardens and Landscapes* and other works.

Casa Urraca Press publishes creative works by authors we believe in. New Mexico and the U.S. Southwest are rich in creative and literary talent, and the rest of the world deserves to experience our perspectives. So we champion books that belong in the conversation—books with the power, compassion, and variety to bring very different people closer together.

We are proudly centered in the high desert somewhere near Abiquiú, New Mexico. Visit us at casaurracapress. com to browse our books and to register for workshops with our authors.

You could smell that café three blocks away, and it made your mouth water. It smelled like rellenos and enchiladas. Hot cheese and chopped onions and bubbling red chile

www.ingramcontent.com/pod-product-compliance
Lightning Source LLC
Chambersburg PA
CBHW032236190726
48289CB00007BA/2409